❤ ❤ ❤

It was **him,** *she thought starkly. Her knight.*

He said she'd been unconscious. Maybe she still was, because the man gripping her arms could have strode straight from her dreams. She *knew* those midnight eyes, the bold slant of his cheekbones, the exotic hollowing beneath; the carnal promise of that mouth framed by that squared warrior's jaw.

In her dreams he had been vague, veiled, as if a mist had obscured her vision, shifting occasionally to allow tantalizing glimpses. Now it was as if a strong wind had blown the mist away; he was pulled into sharp focus, and he was…overwhelming.

Dear Reader,

What is there to say besides, "The wait is over!" Yes, it's true. Chance Mackenzie's story is here at last. *A Game of Chance,* by inimitable *New York Times* bestselling author Linda Howard, is everything you've ever dreamed it could be: exciting, suspenseful, and so darn sexy you're going to need to turn the air-conditioning down a few more notches! In Sunny Miller, Chance meets his match—in every way. Don't miss a single fabulous page.

The twentieth-anniversary thrills don't end there, though. A YEAR OF LOVING DANGEROUSLY continues with *Undercover Bride,* by Kylie Brant. This book is proof that things aren't always what they seem, because Rachel's groom, Caleb Carpenter, has secrets…secrets that could break—or win— her heart. *Blade's Lady,* by Fiona Brand, features another of her to-die-for heroes, and a heroine who's known him—in her dreams—for years. Linda Howard calls this author "a keeper," and she's right. Barbara McCauley's SECRETS! miniseries has been incredibly popular in Silhouette Desire, and now it moves over to Intimate Moments with *Gabriel's Honor*, about a heroine on the run with her son and the irresistible man who becomes her protector. Pat Warren is back with *The Lawman and the Lady,* full of suspense and emotion in just the right proportions. Finally, Leann Harris returns with *Shotgun Bride,* about a pregnant heroine forced to seek safety—and marriage—with the father of her unborn child.

And as if all that isn't enough, come back next month for more excitement—including the next installment of A YEAR OF LOVING DANGEROUSLY and the in-line return of our wonderful continuity, 36 HOURS.

Leslie Wainger

Leslie J. Wainger
Executive Senior Editor

Please address questions and book requests to:
Silhouette Reader Service
U.S.: 3010 Walden Ave., P.O. Box 1325, Buffalo, NY 14269
Canadian: P.O. Box 609, Fort Erie, Ont. L2A 5X3

BLADE'S LADY
FIONA BRAND

Published by Silhouette Books

America's Publisher of Contemporary Romance

Thank you to coroner Heather Ayrton for supplying me
with all the interesting information on missing persons,
and for telling me what I really wanted to know—
how to make the missing person fit my plot.

 SILHOUETTE BOOKS

ISBN 0-373-27093-3

BLADE'S LADY

Copyright © 2000 by Fiona Walker

Books by Fiona Brand

Silhouette Intimate Moments

Cullen's Bride #914
Heart of Midnight #977
Blade's Lady #1023

FIONA BRAND

has always wanted to write. After working eight years for the New Zealand Forest Service as a clerk, she decided she could spend at least that much time trying to get a romance novel published. Luckily, it only took five years, not eight. Fiona lives in a sub-tropical fishing and diving paradise called the Bay of Islands with her husband and two children.

IT'S OUR 20th ANNIVERSARY!
We'll be celebrating all year,
Continuing with these fabulous titles,
On sale in August 2000.

Intimate Moments

#1021 A Game of Chance
Linda Howard

#1022 Undercover Bride
Kylie Brant

#1023 Blade's Lady
Fiona Brand

#1024 Gabriel's Honor
Barbara McCauley

#1025 The Lawman and the Lady
Pat Warren

#1026 Shotgun Bride
Leann Harris

Special Edition

#1339 When Baby Was Born
Jodi O'Donnell

#1340 In Search of Dreams
Ginna Gray

#1341 When Love Walks In
Suzanne Carey

#1342 Because of the Twins...
Carole Halston

#1343 Texas Royalty
Jean Brashear

#1344 Lost-and-Found Groom
Patricia McLinn

Desire

#1309 The Return of Adams Cade
BJ James

#1310 Tallchief: The Homecoming
Cait London

#1311 Bride of Fortune
Leanne Banks

#1312 The Last Santini Virgin
Maureen Child

#1313 In Name Only
Peggy Moreland

#1314 One Snowbound Weekend...
Christy Lockhart

Romance

#1462 Those Matchmaking Babies
Marie Ferrarella

#1463 Cherish the Boss
Judy Christenberry

#1464 First Time, Forever
Cara Colter

#1465 The Prince's Bride-To-Be
Valerie Parv

#1466 In Want of a Wife
Arlene James

#1467 His, Hers...Ours?
Natalie Patrick

Prologue

Sixteen years earlier, Australia

Eleven-year-old Anna Tarrant clung, wet and shivering, to the log that jutted boldly from the riverbank. The brutal strength of the current pinned her against the thick trunk with such force the breath was pressed from her lungs. Water swirled and tossed icily around her face, threatening to push up into her nostrils, into her mouth—threatening to fill her up, then drag her down.

The sound of her name registered above the pounding rush of the river that usually wound, slow and shallow, through the contoured hills of the Tarrant estate. Anna's head jerked up, eyes straining wildly to see beyond the pitch-black curve of the undercut bank to the night sky, which was thickly studded with stars and awash with the cold light of a full moon. Violent shivers made her teeth clack together like castanets.

Henry de Rocheford. Her stepfather.

He reached down, his hand wavering before her eyes. It was his left hand. She could see the ancient, heavy gold of her father's signet ring on his finger, could almost read the inscription that went with the distinctive Tarrant crest.

Anna stared at the ring with stark misery, and grief for her father shuddered through her small, thin body. She intensified her grip on the log, refusing to reach out to her stepfather. He would let her go.

He would let her be swept away, pulled down into the dark, strong coils of the river. She knew that because, when she had slipped on the muddy bank further upstream while calling for her missing puppy, Toto, Henry's helping hand had sent her plunging into the water.

After an eternity of time, Henry's wavering face and hand were replaced by another's—William, the gardener. His craggy face was crumpled with concern, eyes wide with fear, not empty, like Henry's.

Reaching out to William was another thing entirely. Anna was afraid to release her grip on the tree. She was cold, so cold, her fingers numb. She could no longer feel what she was holding on to. Her mind felt slow, stupid. She was afraid that if she let go with one hand, her whole body might let go, and then she would be snatched away. Gone. Like her father. And now Toto.

She didn't want to die.

Terror exploded deep inside her chest, shoved her heart into overdrive and robbed her lungs of precious oxygen. For a moment she thought she would lose consciousness, and in an act of sheer panic she squeezed her eyes shut and reached out in her mind, seeking the magical inner place she'd found, searching with a sharp-edged desperation for *him*. Her secret friend.

Ever since Mama had married Henry, Anna's secret friend had been there when she needed him, and now she needed him very, very badly. Anna wasn't sure who or what he was. She had decided early on that he wasn't an angel, although, from the shadowy details she'd been able to make out, he was beautiful enough to be one. There was a hum of energy, of excitement, about him that just didn't fit with angel's wings.

He was probably a knight. Her knight.

The sound of her name penetrated the odd, lucid calm that had settled over her. It came again, more urgent this time, and Anna's lids flickered sleepily. She felt dazed, disoriented, caught between the dizzying delight of that inner place and the relentless, numbing power of the river.

William leaned lower, hanging directly over her, and for a moment Anna thought that he might tumble into the river, too. His powerful hand wrapped around her wrist—the heat of it searing—and she realised with a beat of fear just how cold she had become.

Abruptly, she was hauled up the bank, her body leaden as a puppet's. William was talking to her, low words of comfort, as he stripped off his jacket and wrapped her in its blissful warmth.

Henry's face loomed. Fear rocketed through her, and, despite the shattering cold, she went rigid. She could *feel* the anger emanating from him like the spill of cold air from a freezer. She had long since learned to conceal the "oddness" of her senses, but now the strangeness rose up inside her like a primitive cry of warning.

She tried to speak, but her vocal chords were as paralysed as the rest of her. In a convulsive movement, she clamped her arms around William's neck and clung to him as fiercely as she'd clung to the log in the river. He kept hold of her.

As if from a great distance, she heard snatches of Henry's smooth, creamy voice, the rhythm of it rich and soft. Measured. "Tried to save her...as unstable as her mother...needs special care..."

William's voice rumbled deep in his chest, the word "hospital" little more than a vibration.

A whispery sob slipped past the raw tightness binding Anna's throat as she burrowed in against his burly chest, burying her face in the rough folds of his sweater. If she was taken to hospital, she would be safe.

For a while.

She needed him.

Seventeen-year-old Blade Lombard clawed his way out of the dream, breathing hard. For long moments he was rigid, frozen, disorientation robbing him of the simple motor skills required to shove himself free of the tangled mess he'd made of the bed.

Moonlight flooded his room with ghostly white light, spilled starkly over the collapsed pile of books on his desk, the football plunked down in the middle of his geography project, the Walkman he blasted his ears with while he did homework.

With a stifled oath, he catapulted to his feet, strode naked to the window and pushed it wide. The chill of the hardwood floor was an anchor to reality he desperately needed as he braced both hands on the sill and leaned out, gulping in the liquid coolness of the night air. A fitful breeze drifted across his skin, bringing with it the familiar scents of his mother's roses and freshly cut lawn, drying the sweat that slicked him from head to toe.

Blade shook his head in an attempt to clear the lingering sense of urgency, the miasma of despair, that still clung to him like heavy layers of wet clothing.

Even though he was only seventeen, he was already over six feet tall and broad in the shoulders. If he woke up sweating and shaking it should have been from a wet dream, not—his jaw clenched—not because a child had called out to him somewhere inside his head. Not because he could *see* the dark swirl of the water trying to drag her down, know that she was cold, intensely cold, and afraid.

Dammit, if she really did exist outside his dreams, he didn't know what he could do to help. He didn't know where she was, or even who she was.

He was beginning to wonder who *he* was.

All he knew for sure was that the child had been haunting him for the past year, and that she was alone—so alone he could taste it.

Pushing himself away from the window, Blade quartered the room in a silent prowl, not wanting to rouse his brothers, who had rooms on either side of his, but he was too wound up to sleep again just yet.

Oh yeah, there was one other thing he knew for sure, he thought grimly. If he ever told anyone he heard voices inside his head, and that the little girl had become so real to him that he was worried about her, they wouldn't just think he was crazy, they would know it.

Chapter 1

Present day, Auckland, New Zealand

It was raining as Anna left the library, a slow drift of icy drizzle condensing out of darkness, swirling with a ghostly brilliance in the yellowish glare of sodium streetlamps.

She slipped on her raincoat as the heavy double doors were locked behind her and the tall, taciturn man who pulled late shift at the front desk flipped up the hood of his voluminous black coat and hunched into the night like a large, disgruntled bird searching for its roost.

Shoving long tendrils of hair back from her face, Anna strode down the shallow stone steps, gripped her briefcase and mentally prepared herself to be gently soaked before she reached the doubtful sanctuary of her flat.

Habit had her searching the shadows, checking the street, the cars. Nothing was out of the ordinary, but that wasn't how she felt. Tonight she felt spooked, uneasy…haunted.

Despite her tension, a wry smile softened the line of her mouth. Haunted enough to consider that she might actually be cursed with some of the more spectacular preternatural talents of her Montague ancestors, which her grandmother had once regaled her with, along with the glories and history of her ancient, almost extinct family.

Extinct, that was, except for her.

The brief flicker of amusement disappeared. The stark fact that, since the death of her mother, Eloise, just months ago, Anna was the last of the Montague line, and almost the last of her father's family—the Tarrants—also sat uneasily with her tonight, although she didn't usually allow herself the luxury of dwelling on either her loneliness or her isolation.

But then, she didn't often find a notice in the local newspaper declaring her to be legally dead.

A shudder swept her, part remnant of the fear that had shaken through her that morning when she'd read the neat black print, part winter chill. The dank coldness swirled and clung, threatening to penetrate her thin coat and sink in all the way to the bone.

She should have expected something like this. Her stepfather, Henry de Rocheford, had to be as aware as she was of her approaching birthday and what it would mean for both of them. They'd played a cat and mouse game for years, but now Henry had run out of time.

He wanted her dead.

Her stomach lurched. The knowledge still had the power to terrify her.

Henry hadn't succeeded in killing her…yet, but he'd come close several times. The last attempt had been seven years ago, sending her into hiding. Now it seemed he had found a better way. He was trying to dispose of her, legally, before she reached her twenty-seventh birthday and qualified for control of her father's massive mining interests—Tarrant Holdings—which had been held in trust for her.

The situation was tangled, frightening…potentially deadly. De Rocheford was a man of great intellect and power, a handsome, charismatic man with all the outward trappings of a gentleman and the resources of the Tarrant wealth at his fingertips. He was her father's half-brother, and although he had no direct claim on his half-brother's estate, he now controlled the company by virtue of his marriage to Anna's mother shortly after Hugh Tarrant's death.

A passing car sent cold mist pluming off the road, wreathing parked cars in a shimmering, ever-dissolving shroud as the drizzle intensified. Anna quickened her pace, her brisk step sounding oddly flattened, as if the mist and drizzle served to muffle even the sharpest sound. As she passed from the relative brightness of the library car park into the badly lit stretch of sidewalk that bordered Ambrose Park, she had the oddest notion that the night would swallow her whole.

She shouldn't have delayed in the musty warmth of the library, huddling over her research materials, trying to lose herself in the medieval treasure trove of the Crusades, the beauty and the brutality, the rich splendour and intellect that rubbed cheek by jowl with ig-

norance and grinding poverty. It hadn't worked. She
hadn't gotten any further along with the novel she was
writing, all she had gained was a headache and gritty
eyes that she would regret tomorrow, when she had to
spend twelve hours solid on her feet at Joe's Bar and
Grill. Her mind had been consumed with that damned
legal notice and her attempt to contact Tarrant's lawyers earlier in the day.

An attempt that had failed.

Emerson Stevens, the partner who dealt with Tarrant
business, most definitely hadn't been able to see her.
He had been killed in a hit-and-run accident just weeks
before. The receptionist had been pleasant but offi-
cious. If Anna wanted to see anyone else, she would
have to make an appointment. Not surprising, Anna
thought, since she'd turned up in her waitressing uniform—Joe's Bar and Grill emblazoned across her
chest—and given her name as Johnson.

The shabby entrance sign to Ambrose Park loomed,
lit by the solitary spotlight that hadn't been broken or
stolen. The park was pleasant enough to walk across
during daylight hours, but at night it was devoid of all
charm and more likely to hold vagrants than lovers.

A tingling of the nerves down her spine, a cold jab
of awareness, presaged a whisper of sound, the scrape
of a shoe on pavement.

Anna ducked, feinted, felt the rush of air as something passed close to her head. Instinctively, she lashed
out with the briefcase; it connected solidly. There was
a muffled curse, a grunt as whoever had tried to hit her
slipped on the slick concrete and tumbled, almost taking her with him.

A booted foot caught her heavily on one knee. She

flailed, grabbed for balance, almost dropping the briefcase. Her shoulder caught the edge of one of the unevenly plastered pillars that guarded the broad entrance to the park. She reeled, still off balance, and saw the cold gleam of light travel the length of a gun barrel as the man regained his feet.

Time seemed to slow, stop, freeze her in place while her mind groped past a paralysing blankness; then fear slammed through her, and with a gasping breath she plunged into the darkness.

In abrupt contrast to the blankness of just moments ago, thoughts and decisions now tumbled in a frantic cascade. The park was her best option; the trees were closer than any building, the undergrowth thick at the edges. And it was very dark. He couldn't shoot her if he couldn't see her.

Clutching the case to her chest, Anna lengthened her stride, but her sneakers kept losing their purchase, slipping on the wet grass.

She risked a glance over her shoulder. A burst of adrenaline punched hotly through her as she saw the man coming after her and knew this was no ordinary mugging. She stumbled, regained her balance. A sense of unreality gripped her as she passed by the darker outline of a set of swings and a slide—innocent reminders of a childhood that for her had ended brutally in a flooded river.

Oh God. She had allowed herself to become complacent, over-confident—lulled by the knowledge that her twenty-seventh birthday was only weeks away, and then she could end this madness. She had been wrong; she'd been found. Someone had been lying in wait for her.

If it hadn't been for that burst of awareness, honed by years of running and hiding, she would be dead. She knew that as surely as she knew that Henry had set her up.

She had made a mistake. Stupid. *Stupid.*

The notice in the paper had served a purpose other than the obvious legal one; it had also been a ploy to flush her out of hiding. There had been someone watching the lawyer's office; she had been followed from there.

She should have rung Emerson Stevens instead of showing up unannounced, only to be blocked. If she'd rung, she would have found out Emerson was dead, and that there was no point in approaching Stevens, Harrow and Cooper directly yet, because with Emerson gone, there was no-one there who knew her by sight. No-one who would believe that she hadn't died when her car had plunged over a cliff into the sea almost seven years ago. No-one who would give her the time of day without irrefutable evidence of her identity.

It was a catch-22 situation. To establish her identity, she would have to reveal herself, turn herself into a target while the wheels of justice slowly ground their course. If she had to resort to DNA testing to prove her right to her own inheritance, that could take months, and money she didn't have.

Panic grabbed at her insides as the ruthless simplicity of Henry's strategy sank in and eroded her confidence. Henry was nothing if not thorough. Having her declared legally dead would finalise his claim on Tarrant Holdings, then he would make the legal fiction a physical fact by having her disposed of before she had time to establish her identity.

One way or another, the shadowed half life of Anna Johnson-Tarrant would cease.

She heard the pounding of footsteps above her own, caught the edge of a guttural phrase, and panic surged again. The man was gaining. She could hear the grunting rush of his breath as he strained to catch her, almost feel the brush of his fingers as he reached to grab her clothing, a shoulder, an arm. The trees loomed close, closer, then she was among them, branches whipping at her legs, tugging at her clothing as she weaved blindly, more by instinct than sight, because it was like running into a wall of darkness. She wavered, confused, slammed head first into a tree and fell to the ground, stunned.

She rolled and crawled on—the briefcase awkward—thankful that the thick layer of leaves was too sodden to rustle. A rough oath grated, low and harsh. Light dazzled her as the beam of a flashlight swept the trees, flooding the dense brush with an unholy radiance that backlit the short, stocky man who was after her. The beam scythed over her head. She dropped flat, damming her startled breath in her throat, hugging the cold, wet earth like a hungry lover.

After an eon, he moved on. She could hear the uneven thud of his tread—as if he was limping—feel the hot pulse of a lump forming on her forehead, taste blood in her mouth.

Her head spun as she regained her feet and started in the direction opposite from the one the man was taking, feeling her way from tree to tree, lifting and setting her feet down with care. The ground was uneven, an obstacle course of jutting tree roots and slippery vegetation.

The beam swung back, almost silhouetting her. She ducked and crouched behind a tree trunk, holding her breath for long, strained moments. When the beam swung away, she once more hugged her briefcase to her chest and headed for the only source of light she could see, a blue and red glow that she knew emanated from the towering neon Gamezone sign that garishly announced the presence of the video arcade near her flat.

Minutes later, she stumbled free of the trees and stepped into…darkness.

The fall was abrupt, shocking. For long moments she lay unmoving, facedown in what she dimly recognised as the deeply carved groove of a storm drain. The smell of mud and her own fear filled her nostrils; the sound of her racing heart jackhammered in her ears. She still had her briefcase; it was lodged beneath her, its hard edges digging into her stomach, her breasts. She was going to have bruises—lots of them.

Pushing herself onto her hands and knees, she gripped the case and fought to still the sickening spinning in her head. She fingered the tight, tender lump already forming there.

Clutching a fistful of icy grass, she began to climb out of the ditch. She was almost out, so close, when she lost her footing and, hampered by the awkward weight of the case, tumbled back. A sound broke from her throat. Pain flared, as if someone had just driven a thick spike through her skull, then dissolved into swirling shards of darkness.

Just before the blackness claimed her completely, the elusive threads of the old familiar fantasy she used to escape into when she was a child—and sometimes even now, when she dreamed—wound through her mind.

Her knight.

His face shimmered into vague focus: the long hair, black as midnight satin; fierce, dark eyes; the strong chiseled planes and angles of a face that was both grimly handsome and exotically sensual. Oh yeah, he was a fantasy, all right. Why couldn't you be real? she thought hazily.

Right now, the fantasy, pretty as it was, just didn't do the job.

Blade shoved free of the bed. And the dream.

His heart was pounding, his skin damp with sweat, his chest heaving like a bellows. He swore, a low, dark rumble of sound. Dragging unsteady fingers through his hair, he fought to banish the image of mist and rain and darkness. Trees, lots of trees, and a pulsing neon sign. The woman, lying crumpled on the ground, afraid…hunted. A dark bank rearing overhead.

The dream had been strong this time.

A shudder swept him, compliments of the disorientating aftermath of the dream—and other far more potent emotions: his powerful need to intervene, to protect and help her, to push back whatever darkness had hounded first the child, and now the woman with such ferocity that she was somehow propelled into his dreams, his thoughts.

Renewed tension coursed through him. He didn't have a clear idea of what the woman looked like, or her name.

His jaw locked. How he longed to hang a name on her.

If she was real, he reminded himself grimly. Oh baby, if she was real.

Either way, like the other dreams he'd had, Blade had nothing to go on other than the belly punch of the woman's emotions, her desperate thoughts, the stark images that haunted him.

The dreams weren't always about her being attacked, helpless—sometimes they were entirely different.

His breath sifted from between clenched teeth as he pushed a set of bifold doors wide open and stepped naked onto the paved terrace of his penthouse suite at the Lombard Hotel.

A cold, fitful breeze swirled, disturbing the black mane of hair that tumbled to his big shoulders, evaporating the sweat from his skin. He welcomed the ensuing chill that roughened his flesh, made all his muscles tighten.

He stared blindly out at Auckland's version of a winter night, eyes slitted, focused inward, his mind consumed with the woman who consistently invaded his dreams.

Sometimes he made to love to the shadowy woman.

Frustration burned, threatening to erupt into temper. He reined it in. Blade didn't like losing control in any area of his life. This desperate, endless hunger for a woman who existed only in his dreams tormented him, made him helpless in a way he couldn't—wouldn't—tolerate.

Dammit, he didn't even know what she looked like, beyond the fact that she was slim and delicately built, with a silky swath of dark hair that glowed copper in the light, and when he touched her...

A hoarse groan wrenched itself from deep in his

throat. When he touched her, it was like touching fire—
they both burned.

His jaw tightened. The raw need to possess the
woman in his dreams, the flood of pleasure that
swamped him at the simplest of touches, haunted him,
mocked him. He had never felt anything remotely like
it in real life.

Dispassionately, he considered the yawning gulf between the dreams and reality.

His libido was healthy, some might say too healthy,
but he was no sexual predator. The primitive desire to
possess the woman that permeated those sensual encounters was as alien to Blade as the dreams were. The
fact was, he enjoyed women—plural—their friendship
and the sex, but he had never needed any of his sexual
partners beyond the act.

Broodingly, he paced the width of the terrace,
gripped the cold iron of the railing, and faced the disturbing essence of his unease. He wanted the dreams
to be real. More, he *hungered* for what he experienced
in the dreams but had never found anywhere else.
Every time he touched a woman, made love to her, he
was aware that he was grasping for that exquisite, primitive intensity and not finding it.

The breeze kicked up, sending moist air whirling like
a damp cloak about his shoulders. The deepening chill
matched the bleakness of his thoughts. When he was
buried deep inside a woman, he shouldn't have to
feel…alone.

Then there was the matter of control. If he made love
to a woman, he retained control. All the way.

And he never made love with strange women. He
had certain standards, a code of honour that was as

simple and ruthlessly direct as a set of military orders. One of the rules of engagement was that he always insisted on an introduction first.

He began to notice the cold. His breath condensed in the air, mist wreathed the streetlamps below and hung in streamers across the road. It was also drizzling, a light, drifting drizzle.

Like the dream.

Traffic was sporadic, but still steady. He could see couples strolling, maybe catching a movie or supper at one of the street cafes.

It wasn't that late. He had only been asleep for a short time. The dream must have taken hold of him the second his head had hit the pillow. There was an odd jolting sensation he'd come to recognise, as if some internal switch had been thrown. Then the dream unravelled. Images. Impressions. Sometimes nothing but a jumble, sometimes pictures that were startlingly clear. Like tonight.

He cursed as the images replayed themselves in his mind. He remembered the vivid blue and red of the neon sign. The sign had said...

Gamezone.

His head came up, nostrils flaring as if he'd caught an elusive scent, one he'd been seeking for more years than he cared to count. If only to disprove it.

"Gamezone."

He said the name out loud, letting it linger on his tongue, as if testing the veracity of the syllables.

With a harsh exclamation, he strode inside, switched on a lamp and reached for the telephone book.

He was clutching at shadows. Maybe when he came

up with another blank the stranglehold on his gut would ease up.

Despite reason and cold logic, his pulse hammered as he searched through the book, ran his finger down a page…and stopped.

"Son of a bitch."

Blade's heart slammed once, hard, against the wall of his chest. His gaze narrowed at the bold type advertising a games arcade in one of the seedier areas of town, but no matter how hard he looked at the address, it didn't disappear.

Gamezone.

Blade stared at the garish blue and red sign. A sign he remembered but had never *seen*.

His gaze swept the surrounding area, noting the unmistakeable uniformity of state housing jammed cheek by jowl with clusters of badly built apartments. Definitely down at heel.

A darkened area caught his eye. A park.

He called himself crazy, but put the Jeep Cherokee in gear and cruised closer, noting the name of the park, the broken lights, the shabby plastered pillars guarding the entrance. Swinging the Jeep into a space, he pulled on a leather jacket, eased it over the fit of the Glock shoved snug in its shoulder holster, checked the knife in his boot and grabbed a torch, but didn't turn it on.

Thunder rolled, giving a low-register warning of the incoming storm. The strengthening breeze scattered rain in his face, bringing with it scents that were city-tame, others that were earthy, wild. Something equally uncivilised unraveled inside Blade, and despite the fury and frustration that still ate at the edges of his temper, he bared his teeth in a cold grin. He stood by the Jeep for long seconds, his senses animal-sharp as he stared across the expanse of grass and trees with eyes peculiarly well-adjusted to the smothering blackness.

When he'd been with the Special Air Service he'd been called names—he'd been called lots of names—but he couldn't completely deny the wolf's blood that was purported to run in his veins. He felt like howling right now.

He should be tucked up in bed, getting his beauty sleep. Or, better still, tucked up in bed with a beauty and getting no sleep at all. Not hunting a…ghost.

A chill went through him, along with echoes of urgency and the compulsion that had driven him out into the night. He had to check. Gamezone had been real. For his own peace of mind, he had to check.

If *she* was real…

He rejected the thought. She couldn't be real. Better to think about what he was going to do when he didn't find a woman—like which psychiatrist he'd choose to oversee his therapy, and whether or not he should have himself committed.

He searched the area, coldly, efficiently, and found nothing.

Finally he walked the perimeter and found the storm water drain…and his ghost.

Chapter 2

She was lying, curled as defenceless as a baby, amidst grass, mud, crumpled cans and takeaway wrappers.

Her very stillness was chilling. For a moment, Blade thought he was too late and that she was dead, but the first touch told him that wasn't so. The pulse beating at her throat was regular and strong. His ghost was alive, but hurt.

His relief was followed by a short, hard jolt of rage. Blade lived his life on simple terms. He was—or had been, until a few weeks ago—a soldier. In more primitive terms, a warrior. The art of war, the hunt, had been his game. It had excited him as little else had, and he had played it well. But one of his rules had been that women and children had no part in the action. He thought that rule was simple enough even for the bad guys to understand. It ticked him off big time when they didn't.

Gently, he felt down the length of her body, testing for broken bones; then ran his fingertips over her scalp. When he encountered the goose egg in the centre of her forehead, he flicked on the torch, which was taped so that only a thin slit of light played over her pale features.

Long, wet hair was slicked back from a face that was less than beautiful, more arresting than pretty, an intriguing blend of delicacy and strength and Ambrose Park dirt. She was average in height, maybe taller, and despite having the firm muscle tone of someone who either exercised regularly or worked physically hard, she was finely built. Delicate.

Blade's stomach twisted as the description registered, and for a dizzying moment a dream image rose up to overlay that of the woman lying on the ground. Fiercely, he shook it off. A lot of women were slender, finely built; it didn't mean a thing. This woman was real, not a dream.

Cleaned up, he bet she would be something—the kind of woman who should be wearing a slick business suit and sexy high heels, not the loose jeans, sweatshirt and cheap nylon raincoat she was wearing. He put her age at mid-twenties, but something about the taut, moulded shape of her cheekbones and jaw suggested more than the usual strength and character of a woman that age. Even unconscious, there was no softness, just pared-down intensity.

He shook her. She stirred but didn't open her eyes.

Lightning sheeted across the sky, throwing his shadow across the woman and burning her inert form into his retinas with a searing clarity. Thunder rumbled again, and tension coalesced between his shoulder

blades as the rising wind buffeted his back. Too much
noise to hear if whoever had attacked the woman was
still skulking around, and he could do without the lightning.

He shook her again. She groaned, a husky thread of
sound. Her head lolled toward him, and Blade saw the
blood, angling across her temple, trickling down one
of those exquisite cheekbones. Her eyelids flickered,
ridiculously long, velvety lashes lifted, and her blank
gaze fastened briefly on his before she sank back into
unconsciousness.

Anna knew someone was shaking her.

She tried to wake up, but it was like swimming
through molasses, she never quite seemed to make it
to the surface. She was tired—so tired—all she wanted
to do was sleep, but the voice was insistent, low, dark,
with a kind of delicious rumble that she fixed on like
a beacon. The hands that held her were shiveringly hot,
like an electric charge tingling along her arms. The
man, for it was a man, was like fire. The warmth from
his body beat against her chilled flesh in waves, and
that low voice continued to cajole—as soothing, as animal rough, as a purr. It wasn't a voice she'd heard
before, but it was oddly familiar all the same. It caught
her attention and held it, even against the heavy drag
of sleep.

She didn't feel afraid of the voice, although a part
of her wondered distantly at her lack of fear; she was
too busy listening to the rich, dark cadences, the intriguing roughness, and soaking in the beguiling heat
of his hands. She wanted to get closer to that whispery
rumble, the magical heat that seemed to reach out and
enfold her, and she wondered dreamily what it would

feel like, how hot it would be, if she reached out and wrapped herself around *him.*

The tenor of the voice changed, became more urgent. Abruptly, Anna remembered where she was, the danger she was in. She needed to open her eyes, to wake up. Despite her puzzling response to the man, she didn't know the voice, and she couldn't afford to trust it.

Blade tightened his grasp on the woman's shoulders and shook her again, this time more sharply. He wanted her out of here, ASAP. The drizzle had thickened into hard-driving gusts of rain, and he had a nasty itch running up his spine. He didn't know how she had ended up in the storm drain, or who she could possibly be, but he didn't intend for either of them to stay there any longer than they had to. The woman in his dream had been in some kind of trouble, and so had this woman.

It had to be sheer coincidence that he'd found her. City parks were prime spots for trouble of all kinds, especially in areas like this. There would be a logical explanation for her presence that had nothing at all to do with the dreams. He was determined to have that explanation.

Her eyes flickered, opened wide and fixed unblinkingly on him. She went rigid in his grip.

"It's all right." He pitched his voice low. "Someone attacked you. You've been unconscious. I'm going to take you to a hospital."

"No hospital." Her voice was husky, but surprisingly steady.

Anna stared at the man who held her, his large, powerful form crouched over her as he used his body to shield her from the thin, icy rain that whirled in the weak beam of a torch. She struggled to orient herself and failed. She felt as if a giant fist had closed around her heart, her lungs, squeezing until her head spun and she had to fight for breath.

It was *him,* she thought starkly. Her knight.

He said she'd been unconscious. Maybe she still was, because the man gripping her arms could have strode straight from her dreams. She *knew* those midnight eyes, the bold slant of his cheekbones, the exotic hollowing beneath; the carnal promise of that mouth framed by that squared warrior's jaw.

In her dreams he had been vague, veiled, as if a mist had obscured her vision, shifting occasionally to allow tantalising glimpses. Now it was as if a strong wind had blown the mist away; he was pulled into sharp focus, and he was…overwhelming. He should have been clad in dark armour, a helm held carelessly under one arm, his face and hair damp with sweat as he grinned in reckless triumph at another jousting victory. He shouldn't be *here. Now.* He belonged in a hundred other places, a hundred other times—between the pages of the novel she was writing.

She wondered if she *had* conjured him up, if the shock and strain of running from the man who had attacked her, the blow to her head, had affected her mind.

If she was hallucinating, the illusion was nice, she decided a little giddily. Very detailed. Better than the fuzzy images of her dreams, or anything she had ever imagined or committed to a page.

Deliberately, she inhaled, and caught the scents of mud and grass and rain, and the faint drift of something far more potent—warm male and damp leather. The scent of him grounded her with a thump.

He was here. She wasn't dreaming. Whoever the stranger was, he was real.

His gaze was steady on her, piercing in the dim glow from his torch. "I need to get you out of the rain, and you need a doctor," he murmured, his voice deep, laced with that smoky rumble.

The sound of it rippled down her backbone, tightened the tender skin at her nape in a primitive shiver of warning.

His hand lifted to her face, fingertips searingly hot against her jaw. "If you can't walk, I'll carry you."

Anna grasped his hand, disconcerted at the sharp thrill of sensation as his fingers closed over hers, aware that the pads of his fingers and palm were rough and calloused instead of city-soft.

"No hospital," she repeated as evenly as she could manage, given that her heart was still pounding with the aftershock of her discovery, fanciful or not, and a heavy jolt of what she could only label as acute awareness of the man holding her. "I—stumbled and fell. Hit my head. It's just a bump, I…" She took a breath and pulled herself into a sitting position, wincing as her head spun anew. "I can walk. My briefcase. I need my briefcase."

"It's here."

The relief as her fingers closed over the familiar grip was almost too much. "Good," she said numbly, unable to prevent the tremor that shook through her. "That's good."

She couldn't risk losing her briefcase. Everything that mattered to her was in it. Her laptop computer and diskettes. The notes for her book. Enough cash that if she had to, she could walk away from her shabby little apartment without her possessions and have enough to survive on until she found another place to live and a new job. Most important of all were the contents of her handbag when she had run all those years ago: credit cards, a driver's licence, the passport she'd never been able to use. Over the years she'd also amassed a collection of faded newspaper and magazine cuttings— every time some journalist resurrected the mystery of the missing Tarrant heiress, the unstable young woman who had thrown away a life of wealth and privilege in the most flamboyant of gestures, by supposedly driving her expensive sports car over a cliff.

The documents and photos weren't conclusive proof of her identity—she could have stolen them—but she clung to them; they were hers. She had changed—her breath caught in her throat when she thought of just how much she had changed—but the strong resemblance in those photos was all she had. When she'd stumbled, bruised and bleeding, from her wrecked car all those years ago, she had simply picked up her purse and run. She'd had the clothes on her back, the jewellery she had been wearing and some cash. She hadn't dared use the credit cards.

She had escaped Henry's last, clever attempt on her life by sheer blind luck. When her car's brakes had failed, a tree had been all that had stopped a certain plunge over the cliff's edge into the water far below.

Her utter helplessness in the face of her stepfather's relentless determination to remove her from his path had almost paralysed her with fear; but she had known in that moment that she couldn't afford to stay around—certainly not until she was twenty-seven—and give him another opportunity to kill her. When she'd later discovered that Henry had decided to cut his losses and had pushed her car over the cliff, making it look like she'd died, she had known she'd made the right decision.

She hadn't gone to the police. She had already tried that avenue, and no one had listened. She'd been twenty years old, and Henry had seen to it that her credibility was less than zero. He had painted a convincing picture of a hysterical young woman balanced on the edge of mental instability. He had done a great job of character assassination, and she had played into his hands on several occasions by openly accusing him of trying to murder her, from the age of eleven on. It had been a case of people thinking she was crying wolf. Even her own mother had believed she was mentally unstable.

Until the sabotage on her car's brakes, Anna had begun to believe it herself.

No one had given credence to the notion that Henry de Rocheford was doing anything more than looking out for the interests and welfare of the Tarrant family, as he had "selflessly" done for years.

She had to wonder if anyone would now.

Minutes later, they were standing in the shadow of the entranceway to the park.

Anna's wet coat clung and dragged. Moisture was seeping through in several places, and she was shivering, but she didn't protest; she wanted to check the street before she stepped out onto it.

Despite the fact that she'd insisted she was capable of walking, she felt disconcertingly weak and was sharply aware that she was in no shape to handle anything else the night might throw at her. She swayed, her hand groping for the rough surface of one of the stone pillars for support, and didn't protest when the stranger wrapped his arm around her waist, clamping her close against his side. The solid barrier of his body protected her from much of the wind and rain, and the heat that poured from him drove back the worst of the chill. Anna stiffened at her ready acceptance of the stranger's protection, the extent of her trust in him when she didn't trust anyone, the disturbing memory of those moments when she'd actually wanted to get closer to him. The bump on her head must have skewed her judgement.

His voice vibrated close to her ear, making her jump. "Where do you live?"

Anna didn't bother to dissemble. "I have a flat nearby." There was no point in not telling him where. She would have to leave, anyway. Tomorrow.

"I'll see you home."

The statement was delivered flatly, and she wasn't inclined to argue with it. The stranger was big, well over six feet tall, and from what she had seen and could feel, he was solidly muscled. His arm tightened around her as he urged her across the road to a Jeep.

He helped her into the passenger seat. The Jeep smelled new and expensive. For the first time, it occurred to Anna to question what a well-heeled stranger had been doing strolling through Ambrose Park in the rain, at night, and what had compelled him to even look in the storm drain?

She knew he wasn't the man who had chased her earlier; he was too tall, for one thing. But what if he *had* been looking for her? She couldn't discount that possibility, no matter how much she wanted to trust him.

He swung into the driver's seat with a sleek, fluid grace that drew her gaze. He had taken his jacket off, and in the dimly lit confines of the cab, his muscled biceps gleamed copper as he twisted and placed the dark bundle in the rear, along with the torch he'd carried. In the short time it had taken him to remove the jacket, his T-shirt had gotten soaked, and now it clung slickly to his broad shoulders and chest.

With dawning apprehension, she realised just how big, how powerfully built, he was, and that he was dressed completely in black: black pants, black boots— even a black watch, with a cover hiding the face. The colour of thieves and assassins.

His hair was long, caught back in a ponytail. She hadn't noticed that in the dark; she had assumed his hair was short. Anna swallowed, for a moment caught again in the hazy limbo between sleep and wakefulness that had swamped her when she'd regained consciousness. This was no dream, she told herself fiercely. And he was no knight in shining armour, despite the fact that he'd helped her.

She tipped her head back to meet his gaze, and her breath hitched in her throat despite her attempts at control. His eyes were as dark as his clothing, an intense shadow-black that seemed to absorb light, giving nothing back. The effect was sombre, electrifying.

The impact of his face hit her all over again, sending an odd quiver of mingled fear and elation through her, starting a queer shifting sensation deep in her stomach, as if her centre of gravity had just altered and she hadn't yet found her balance. Heat rose in her as she

experienced another heavy jolt of the awareness that
had disoriented her so badly earlier, as if she were once
more caught in the relentless grasp of one of the vividly
sensual dreams that had haunted her through the years.

Abruptly, she transferred her gaze to the rain-washed
windscreen. Cold logic and bitterness dashed ice on the
mystifying, aching flare of emotion. Whatever improbable fantasies had played through her mind when she'd
first seen him, they were just that: improbable. She no
doubt had a mild concussion, and her mind was playing
bizarre tricks on her. The guy was big, tough and drop-
dead gorgeous; he would have women queueing. She
wasn't in the market for a relationship, and even if she
were, she had absolutely no confidence in her ability
to handle a man like him.

He shoved the key in the ignition; the engine rumbled to life. ''Where to?'' His gaze locked briefly with
hers.

''Second left. Finnegan Street. Number fifty-four.''

Anna felt the touch of his gaze again; then he was
all business, checking for traffic as he eased onto the
road.

''If I had been going to hurt you, I would have done
it back there,'' he stated flatly, his voice like dark vel-
vet.

Pitched just that way to soothe her, she thought, realising just how tightly she was wound, just how para-
noid her thoughts had become. ''If I thought you would
hurt me, I wouldn't be sitting here.''

And it was the truth, she realised, startled at how
bone-deep that trust had gone. Mysterious though he
was to her, she couldn't shake the extraordinary compulsion to trust him.

Seconds later, he pulled over outside her block of flats.

"Thank you." She aimed a grateful look in his general direction, fumbled her door open, then almost cried with frustration when her briefcase caught under the dash, slowing her escape.

He was already swinging out, striding around to help her down. He gripped her elbow, steadying her when she almost fell—and another of those quivering shocks travelled up her arm. It was too much. She jerked free, stumbling back, almost oblivious to the cold, steady rain streaming down her face, penetrating the collar of her raincoat and trickling down her neck.

He was talking to her, that smoky, soothing rumble again, as if he were trying to gentle a wild animal. She stared at him blankly for long seconds, not comprehending a word he was saying.

He held both hands up, palms out, in a gesture that cut through her confusion and suddenly made her feel foolish. He had only been trying to help her.

Mortified heat warmed her cheeks. He'd sheltered and protected her, driven her home—his actions those of a man used to caring for women, used to handling them. If he hadn't grabbed her just then, she would have fallen.

"I'm sorry, I'm not..." She stopped, feeling even more clumsy, more inept. Not what? she thought bleakly. Not used to kindness? Not used to men touching her?

"You're shaken. You've got a head injury. All I want to do is see you safely inside." His mouth quirked at one corner. "Out of the rain."

The rain. God, the rain. They were both getting

soaked. She drew a breath. "Okay." With a nod that she instantly regretted, she started up the cracked concrete path.

Anna paused at the door to her apartment, which was little more than a one-room bedsit. She turned to thank him, but he forestalled her.

"I know you don't trust me, but I'm not leaving until you've either called a doctor or you let me take a look at that bump on your head."

Once again, Anna was struck with confusion. The mere thought that anyone wanted to help her, take care of her, was so alien that for a moment she couldn't take it in. She fingered the swelling, flinching at the hot bite of pain. Her fingers came away streaked with blood. "You're a doctor?" She didn't try to hide her disbelief.

Blade curbed the desire to reach out and try to soothe her with touch. It wouldn't work, he decided dispassionately. She was as jumpy as a cat with its paw caught in a trap, and just as likely to lash out at him. It wouldn't take much for her to kick him out on his ass, and he couldn't allow that to happen. Not until he'd found out the answers to some questions. "I've had medical training. I was in the military until a couple of months ago. 'Combat' medicine."

For a moment, Blade thought she wasn't going to go for it, and he was knocked off balance by another emotion entirely—one he wasn't pleased to admit to. Something about his ghost caught at his gut, grabbed him deep and hard. He felt…proprietary, protective. He had found her, and he was responsible for her. He wasn't willing to let her go just yet.

When she put her case down and began digging for

her key in her raincoat pocket, relief and satisfaction uncurled inside him. She didn't want to, but she was going to trust him.

His gaze narrowed as he noted the strain she was still under, and the unusual control she was exerting now, despite the scare she'd just had. She should be shaking, coming apart, and he should be comforting her, lending her a shoulder to cry on if that was what she wanted—but none of those things were happening.

He didn't know what this woman needed beyond a painkiller and rest. She wasn't asking for his attention, and, even though she'd given him a measure of trust, he'd had to prise it from her. She would snatch it back in a second if he gave her reason.

She inserted the key in the lock, pushed the door open, stepped inside and flicked a switch. The small, sparse room flooded with the dim light of a naked, low-wattage bulb. Blade followed her in, cataloguing the room in one smooth sweep, noting windows and doors—the action as natural to him as it was to carry the Glock he'd left folded up in his jacket in the Jeep.

His persona shifted from soldier to male as she set the briefcase down beside her tiny dining table and began unbuttoning her coat.

He'd already noted that she was slim; now he saw that she could stand to gain a few pounds, although he knew there were curves beneath those shapeless clothes. When he'd helped her from that ditch, she must have had a dizzy spell, because she'd stumbled. For a split second she'd gone boneless against him and he'd felt the firm pressure of her breasts against his stomach.

She was also shivering and pale, her eyes big in her

face. Too damn big. They were an odd colour, a strange, riveting, silver-grey, as if mist and shadows had taken up permanent residence there.

And her mouth… Something kicked hard in his gut. He hadn't noticed her mouth before, but now that she'd wiped off some of the mud, it took all of his attention. It was pale, lush, pretty and sultry. Grimly, he logged the growing tension in his groin as he closed the door behind him. Oh, yeah…in other circumstances, he would want that mouth.

She bent to unfasten the last button, and in the light, her wet spill of hair, which he now saw was caught back in some loose, intricate braid, took on a warmer hue. Blade stared, transfixed both by the length of her dark hair and by its coppery gleam. When it was dry, it would be a silky veil, cloaking her shoulders, falling past her waist.

Hit number two, he thought bleakly. She was delicately made, and she was a redhead. Now all he had to do was find out what she was running from, and whether or not she had a history of…unusual dreams.

Anna began to shrug out of her coat. She flinched, startled, as her rescuer helped her the rest of the way and then looped the coat over the hook on the back of the door. The easy, matter-of-fact way he carried out that small courtesy caught her attention. She had been right when she'd thought he was used to taking care of women, of handling them. The gesture had been pure gentleman, but the easy way he'd assumed she would let him take care of her had been one hundred percent male.

He studied her forehead, frowning. "You look like you've been in a fight. How did you say you got that?"

Anna tried to remember exactly what she'd told him, but her mind was a frustrating blank. The impression her rescuer had made on her was so vivid that she had trouble recalling anything but him. She decided to stick with the truth as far as she could. "Ran into a tree."

His fingers skirted the edges of the bump, and her insides lurched, both at the tenderness of the bruised area and her tingling awareness of his slightest touch.

"Hate to see the tree," he murmured.

That surprised a laugh out of her. The laugh hurt—as well as amazed her—and she groaned, lowering herself gingerly onto the single, hard-backed chair pulled up next to the table.

She heard him moving in the kitchenette. Heard her ancient fridge door reluctantly give way to the pressure of his hand, then suck closed with a tight-fisted finality, as if grudgingly giving up some of its meagre contents. A sharp sound had her eyes blinking wide in time to witness the brief tussle as he extracted ice from a frosted-up tray. A cube flipped out, evaded the snaking reach of his big hand and hit the floor. He swore as it skidded away, caught her eye and grinned.

In the dim light of her flat, his teeth were white against his skin—the wide smile so unexpected that she felt like he'd clubbed her with it.

Anna couldn't drag her gaze from the mesmerising flash of amusement and what it did to the strong, utterly male contours of his face. She swallowed, abruptly stricken by a sense of isolation, of removal from the human condition, so intense that she had to fight the need to curl in on herself and weep. She couldn't remember the last time she'd shared something as intimate, as silly, as that moment with the ice-cube—let alone the grin. Now that lack stunned her. She felt the deprivation as a piercing ache that drove deep, then burst outward, resolving into a twitching shiver that lifted all the fine hairs at her nape. She was starving for human contact, human warmth, and the knowledge filled her with desperate fear.

She had to pull herself together, and quickly. She was wary of any and all strangers, and had no friends to speak of. She lived this way for a good reason: to stay alive. To feel what she was feeling—this wild, famished hunger for a touch, a smile, from a man she had never met before and would never see again—was beyond odd; it was crazy.

"What's your name?" Her demand was raspy, hollow, even to her own ears. She didn't care. Suddenly it seemed very important that, if nothing else, she should have his name.

"Blade."

He went down on his haunches beside her, and her awareness of the hot sensuality that was as much a part of him as that big-cat grace shuddered through her in another aching wave, as if she were caught in the grip of a fever. He'd wrapped the ice in a tea-towel, and now he gently pressed it to her forehead. All the while, he watched her with an intensity that was blatantly male, speculative, and that made her feel unbearably aware of her own femininity—something she had avoided thinking about for a very long time.

"Blade Lombard," he finished softly.

Anna froze. Lombard. She blinked, for a moment unable to move beyond this new shock. She knew him. Or, at least, she had known him in another place, another lifetime, when she'd been a child.

A flash of memory surfaced, pitched and rolled with a disorienting sense of deja vu. Before her father died, they had lived in Sydney and moved in the same social stratosphere as the Lombards. Of course, Blade had been older—a lot older, to the five- or six-year-old child she'd been—close to adult status in her eyes. She remembered falling off a bike, and Blade helping her up. He'd comforted her, made her sit in a chair, just like this, while he cleaned her knee and applied a dressing. All the while, he'd resisted the taunts of the other children, bending all of his attention on her.

Would he remember her? she wondered on a beat of despair. And what would she do if he did? Could she risk revealing her identity to him?

The Lombards had had business connections with her father. She could vaguely remember, if not their actual faces, their occasional presence at social gatherings. She wondered if Tarrant Holdings still did business with the Lombards, if Blade and her stepfather were partners in some deal, if Blade was a potential threat to her?

She didn't dare find out.

The incongruity of Blade Lombard strolling through Ambrose Park at this time of night, or any time—of even being in the vicinity of this rough neighbourhood—struck her more forcibly. Something was wrong. It didn't fit. He shouldn't have been there.

No. She couldn't trust him, no matter how much she wanted to.

Her hand automatically rose to her face, as if she could shield herself from him. When she realised what she was doing, her fingers curled, forming a fist, and she let her hand fall back into her lap.

Blade didn't miss the wild dilation of the lady's pupils, her sharp intake of breath, although both reactions could have been attributed to the cold pain of the ice-pack settling against her forehead.

He didn't think so. She knew who he was.

Not that recognition was entirely unexpected. Occasionally, some hack reporter got bored for news and sniffed around the Lombard family. The Lombard hotel chain was high profile by necessity, but some of the personal storms his family had weathered had turned into media circuses, adding a certain glamour and notoriety to the Lombard name. Like it or not, they were known.

"And your name?" he demanded quietly.

She stared at him, grey eyes as blank and opaque as a wall of mist.

"Anna Johnson," she said, without hesitation or inflection, and Blade knew beyond all doubt that his ghost lady was lying.

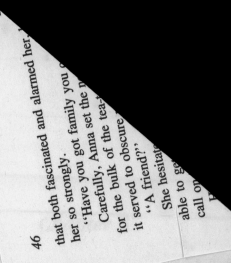

that both fascinated and alarmed her
her so strongly.

"Have you got family you
Carefully, Anna set the
for the bulk of the tea-
it served to obscure
"A friend?"
She hesita
able to ge
call o

Anna let ou ...naky sigh when Blade left her holding the ice against her forehead while he went in search of painkillers.

The piercing quality of his gaze had been so unsettling, she had almost given in and told him her real name. For the first time in years, the lie had seemed deceitful, rather than necessary armour against de Rocheford.

He handed her a glass of water and a couple of Paracetamols, then shifted away to lean one hip against the kitchen counter. Arms folded across his chest, he watched her swallow the pills and drink the water.

His steady regard was unnerving. The plain fact was that this room had always been small, but Blade made it seem claustrophobically tiny. It wasn't just his size, although that was intimidating in itself. It was that he seemed larger than life, brimming with a male power

because he drew

an contact?'' he asked.

ow empty glass down, glad

owel wrapped in ice, because

part of her face. ''No.''

d. If she gave him a name, she might be

rid of him sooner. ''If I need help, I can

Tony, from the flat above.''

e frowned. ''Boyfriend?''

The sheer ludicrousness of the suggestion made her smile. Tony Fa'alau wasn't an old man, but he was somewhere north of his fifties, tall and soft-spoken, with a limp. He often turned up at the library and walked her home, but tonight was one of the nights he helped his son, Mike, with security at the video parlour. ''No.''

''Good.''

Her heart skipped a beat at the deliberate way he held her gaze, the satisfaction inherent in that one word.

''But you should still see a doctor. I could take you.''

His tone was neutral, but she could feel the relentless, underlying force of his will. He was a man used to taking charge, used to giving orders. With a sense of amazement, she realised he would take her over completely if she let him. ''It's only a bump on the head. Believe me, this one's not so bad, I've had worse.'' She stopped, aware that on top of everything else, she now had to squash the urge to confide in him.

''Someone hit you?'' he demanded softly.

He didn't move from his semirelaxed position, but Anna was aware of the change in him. His gaze on her had sharpened, and the relaxed pose was no longer indolent.

"No! I—that is, I was…accident-prone as a child."

The intensity of his regard didn't lessen. "What kind of accidents?"

The killing kind.

Anna closed her eyes briefly against the throbbing pain that thought elicited. "I had a couple of nasty falls that ended in concussions."

She rose to her feet, setting the now melting icepack down on the table, forestalling any further questions, hoping he would take the hint and leave. Her head didn't spin, and her legs no longer felt like limp noodles. The rest and the ice had helped, and soon the pills would ease the pain even further.

Blade took the hint, but in order to get to the door, he had to pass right by her. He stopped, one hand on the door handle, close enough that she had to reluctantly tilt her head to meet his gaze. Close enough that she realised with a sense of shock that he was more than just damp, he was wet through; that all the time he had cared for her, his clothes had been clinging to his skin. Even as she watched, a droplet of water trailed down his temple, but he ignored it.

"I'm glad you don't have a boyfriend," he said bluntly, "but I don't like it that you're alone tonight. I'll leave now, because you're out on your feet. You need to rest. But I'll be back tomorrow to check on you. Do you work during the day?"

Anna thought that was a slightly unusual way to phrase the question. Most people worked during the day. "Yes," she said, not supplying him with any details.

The omission didn't seem to bother him. "I'll take you out for dinner, then."

Anna blinked at the flat statement, wondering if she'd heard wrong. Now she was completely confused. Dinner? That sounded like a date.

Again, her lack of reply didn't seem to bother him. He lifted a hand, brushed a strand of hair back from her forehead and stared critically at the bump. She drew a breath at the strange tingling heat of his touch, that odd internal jolt, but forced herself to stay very still when he transferred his attention to her eyes, staring intently into first one, then the other.

"Your pupils look fine," he murmured. "No uneven dilation. How's the headache?"

"I recognise the beat."

His mouth kicked up at one corner in a slow smile that did bad things to her heart rate. "I've heard it a time or two myself."

He left in a swirl of damp air, his dark form merging so perfectly with the night that he seemed to dissolve into darkness rather than simply walk through it. Anna shut the door firmly behind him. Her fingers shook so badly, it took several attempts to hook the chain and drive the bolt home.

Too late, she thought blankly. Way too late on more than one count. She should have refused to let him inside.

He had seen through her. When he had questioned her, she'd been as transparent as glass, reeling from the twin blows of the incident at the park and her rescue by someone she knew.

Not to mention her state of disorientation. Usually she had no problems making judgments about people, but her instincts seemed to have gone completely haywire. Maybe that was so because Blade's uncanny resemblance to the man in her dreams had somehow triggered the wild fantasy, so that for a time she had become hopelessly tangled between dreams and reality. The strange burst of heat, the charge of awareness whenever he had touched her, had kept her off balance. She had never felt anything like it—not even in dreams.

Leaning against the door, she pressed the heels of her hands into both eyes, trying to alleviate the gritty sting, the hot ache buried at both temples. The silence of the room slowly sank in, easing some of her tension. She had survived the attack, and she was still in one piece…more or less.

Reaction hit with the suddenness of a locomotive smashing into a concrete abutment. A low sound tore from her throat, and she wound her arms around her middle, hanging on tight as shudders jerked through her.

She had been found!

This time it had taken months and, unlike all the other times, there had been no warning, no quick word from a neighbour or co-worker telling her that someone was asking after her, or watching her flat. And this time someone had come to her rescue.

The memory of her childish pleas to an imaginary knight to rescue her surfaced, and she stiffened, pushing herself away from the support of the door.

"Get real," she muttered into the quiet emptiness of her room.

Blade Lombard might resemble the knight of her dreams, he might even act like him, but there had been a seasoned edge of danger evident in those cool, black, marauder's eyes. In ancient times he might well have been a knight, but he would have disdained spending his time hanging around at court or even participating in tourneys. He would have gained his experience in the heat of battle.

He'd said he had worked for the military, and she believed him. She was willing to bet he'd spent his time in the special forces. It would fit that ruthless competence, the easy way he'd taken charge.

He had helped her out, but if he'd been in Ambrose Park merely by chance, any interest he had in her could only be motivated by his sense of responsibility toward the lone female he had rescued, nothing more. She couldn't question his chivalry or his manners—they were self evident—but that didn't change what he was. Trouble.

Any woman who spent time with Blade Lombard would automatically attract attention to herself simply by being in his company. She couldn't afford to be noticed, and she definitely couldn't afford to have her photo published in any papers or magazines.

Gingerly, Anna stripped off her damp clothing, trying not to move her head any more than she had to. Her coat had kept off the worst of the rain and mud, but her jeans were soaked to the knees, and her sweatshirt was damp in places where her coat had let the water in. After slipping on a pair of baggy sweatpants and a sweater, she sat on the edge of the bed and bent forward to pull on fleecy socks. The motion made her head pound harder, and she straightened up, holding still, waiting out the ache.

Abruptly she was overcome by a barrage of images: the attack on the sidewalk, the outline of her assailant falling, cold light sliding along the length of a gun barrel. She began to shake again, despite the warm clothing, every muscle in her body rigid with tension.

She should be crawling into bed, pulling the covers over her head and sleeping, but she couldn't afford to do that yet. She had to think, had to move. The man who had attacked her was still out there. He had been limping, which was probably why he had given up the search. He would be back, and it wouldn't take him long to discover where she lived.

She would have to pack before she went to bed; make decisions about which of her meagre possessions she would take with her. *That* wouldn't take long. She could only take what she could carry or load into the large pack she kept beneath the bed.

The following afternoon, Blade turned from the slice of Auckland's bustling seaport that was visible from his office window to catch the eye of the man seated across from his desk. "You're telling me she doesn't exist?"

Jack McKenna, one of Lombards' most senior executives and more family than employee, shook his head. "Nope. I'm telling you that *legally* she doesn't exist. No birth certificate, passport or driver's licence. No records of insurance, mortgages or bank accounts. No criminal record. Not even a parking ticket. *Nada.* Nothing."

"So, Anna Johnson *is* a false name."

Blade had suspected as much, but the reality still annoyed him. She'd met his gaze with those haunted grey eyes of hers, and she had lied.

Jack shrugged. "Easy enough to do, so long as she doesn't own anything that requires record keeping—a house, a car, a bank account. She probably works for cash under the table, so there are no employment or tax records, and pays for any purchases with cash. There are plenty of employers willing to pay slave wages for an employee who'll work all hours without complaint."

The door popped open. Jack's wife, Milly, who doubled as his personal assistant, strode into the room, vivid in a pants suit in some tropical print that was vibrant with blues and oranges. Somehow the colours didn't clash with her red hair. Blade knew that Milly was forty-something, around the same age Jack was, but she looked closer to thirty.

She slapped some papers down on the desk, almost taking Jack's nose off in the process. "Here's the guest list for that charity bash on Saturday. Every man and his dog are gonna be there, including the Prime Minister."

"Thank you," Jack said meekly.

Milly planted her hands on her hips. "Don't flash those blue eyes at me, Jack McKenna. You are not the flavour of the month."

"No, ma'am."

"In a few months time, you will be even less the flavour of the month."

Jack rose to his feet, placed his hands on either side of Milly's face and kissed her. When he was finished, he sat back down.

"Humph." Milly glared at her husband, but Blade noticed the way her gaze lingered wistfully on the rumpled front of his shirt.

Before Jack met Milly, he had been obsessively neat. The knife-edge crease in his suit pants and his exquisite taste in ties had been a by-word in the business world. His ties were now definitely anarchistic, and he was frequently rumpled these days.

Milly strode out. The door closed firmly behind her.

Jack grinned and kicked back in his chair.

Blade's brows went up; he didn't think he had ever seen Jack so happy, or so satisfied, despite Milly's bad temper. "Trouble in marital heaven?"

"Milly's pregnant," Jack said baldly. "She says it's all my fault."

Blade stared thoughtfully at the door, which Milly hadn't quite slammed. He knew that she already had three grown children from a previous marriage. "Takes two to tango."

"Amen to that. It was the tropical honeymoon that did it. She said I ought to be able to control her baser impulses. What can I say?" he murmured, picking up the papers Milly had brought in. "I tried."

Restlessly, Blade paced the length of his office, halting in front of another bank of windows, this one facing into the city. He stared in the general direction of Joe's Bar and Grill, the name that had been emblazoned on the front of Anna Johnson's sweatshirt.

He shoved his hands in his pockets and tried to keep a lid on the wild impatience that was eating away at his usual control. He should forget about her and turn his mind back to work—God knows, there was enough for him to do.

After spending several years with the Special Air Service, Blade had decided it was past time for him to take his place in the family business. He was almost thirty-four, and while he'd been injured twice on operations, once seriously, he counted himself lucky. No point in pushing that luck any further.

The construction of the casino and a retail complex was a massive undertaking. He and Jack were splitting the load between them. The risk involved in setting up the casino and the huge propensity for trouble it represented appealed to Blade far more than becoming involved in some of Lombards' more conventional enterprises, and his family knew it; by nature, he was more conqueror than manager. At the same time, Blade was building his own dream further north, a quarter-horse stud on a wild piece of country caught between high, muscular hills and the Pacific Ocean. The property was remote enough—courtesy of the physical barrier of the hills—to be its own kingdom, yet close enough to Auckland to make for a reasonable commute. After years of travelling, he needed his own base. He was ready to settle down.

Instantly, his thoughts turned back to Anna. He frowned at both the way his mind had made the switch and the string of coincidences she represented.

She would probably be at work now, despite the fact that she should be resting. Her head would be throbbing, feet aching. She would be working for a damn pittance. He should let her get on with it.

If she was still there.

The thought slid into his mind as slick and easy as a knife. Anna was using a false name. She was as jumpy as a cornered cat, and she had been attacked.

He was certain that she was on the run from something. Or someone.

She could be married and running from a husband.

The thought curled into his mind with the sour, savage taint of sexual jealousy. Blade's jaw tensed. If he'd walked into a brick wall in broad daylight, he couldn't have been more astounded. Jealousy. The emotion was alien, unsettling. As intrusive as the dreams. He enjoyed women, and he was naturally possessive, but he had never been *jealous*.

He remembered the softness of Anna's breasts pressing against him when she'd scrambled out of that storm drain, and the thought that she might be tied in some way to another man filled him with fury.

He came from a long line of males who were used to taking what they wanted, and right now he wanted Anna. His genetic heritage was underlined by his name. Every few generations in the Lombard family, someone lost their head and named one of their sons Blade, after the original marauding rogue who had reaved and plundered, carving out the basis of the first Lombard fortune with raw muscle and the help of his trusty blade.

He fingered the ancient earring that pierced his lobe. The small cabochon ruby was said to have belonged to the first Blade and was traditionally passed down to whoever carried the name. He doubted this was the original gem—that had probably been lost in the mists of time—but it was certainly old.

Grimly, he wondered if his ancestor had had the same trouble with women that he himself was now having. If so, he could understand why he'd carved such a bloody swath through history. He had been a frustrated man.

Blade surveyed the bustling cityscape and let the irrational urgency that had chewed his patience to the bone have its way.

What if she *was* the woman in his dreams?

For the first time, he allowed himself to examine the possibility. He remembered how she'd looked last night: eyes wary with secrets, the exquisite curve of her cheekbones, and that pale, sultry mouth.

The primitive hunger that persistently invaded his dreams stirred to life. His jaw clenched against the hot flood of arousal and, more, an intense need to simply have her near.

He might have difficulty believing in anything with a supernatural bent, but he trusted his instincts, and he trusted his body's reactions. He had never felt such a powerful physical response to a woman outside of his dreams. He fiercely resented the loss of control—giving in to the hunger went against the very essence of who and what he was. And yet, he was honest enough to admit that, in part, that was where the heady excitement lay.

The dichotomy should alarm him. It should scare the hell out of him. Instead, he felt a savage exaltation. He wasn't prepared to admit that he had found his dream woman, but he *had* found a woman who touched him on some primitive level in a way he needed to be touched.

He might not understand much about what was happening, or why, but for Blade the problem had just been simplified. He understood his own burning sexuality very well, and when he needed a woman, his approach was time-honoured and straightforward: he went out and got her.

He spun on his heel. Jack was still lounging in a chair, watching him with an amused grin. Blade had forgotten he was in the room. "I'm going out."

"I can see that."

Blade's smile was rueful, edged. "I don't know when I'll be back."

"Believe me, I understand. Take all the time you need."

Chapter 4

Anna hung up the pay phone, relief making her weak. She had finally found a room in a boarding house, although the cost of the bond would come close to cleaning her out financially.

She checked her watch, saw that she'd exceeded the fifteen minutes she had for a break, and started back toward the restaurant, her mind swiftly calculating all that she had to do and how quickly she would have to move. Just a few more hours and she could leave.

Sunlight flashed, diamond bright, off the side mirror of a nearby car. Her eyes squeezed shut to ward off the stab of pain and what it did to the throbbing at her temples.

As she reached the staff entrance of Joe's Bar and Grill, the sunlight was abruptly smothered by heavy gloom. She glanced at the purplish-black thunderheads seething above, rain-rich and roiling with violent energy. She could smell the moisture in the air, feel the tension of the approaching storm.

More rain. Great, just what she needed when she had to shift out of her flat, she thought, as she strode inside, automatically bracing herself against the mental assault of working at Joe's.

At least the lunch rush was well over. If Joe's ever had a lull, this was it, the brief hiatus before the evening trade picked up, although the liquor licence ensured that the huge barnlike restaurant and bar was never empty.

Joe's specialised in bad coffee, fast food and even faster beer, and attracted a clientele that was definitely on the seamy side. The sweeping wooden counter lined with stools emphasised where the money was made. The companionable wail of rhythm and blues soothed patrons into parting with that money even faster, and the pool room off to the side enticed swaggering groups of brash young men to stay until they were flat broke.

The mock saloon doors swished open on a low rumble of thunder, and Anna was glad her tray was safely set down on a table as Blade Lombard stepped into Joe's as casually as if he ate there every day.

He was dressed for business in a suit made of some dark, fine material. The jacket fitted his broad shoulders like a supple, expensive glove. His gauzy grey collarless shirt was open at the throat and had probably cost the equivalent of a month's worth of her wages. He looked wealthy, sleek and dangerous, and as out of place at Joe's as an exotic jungle cat prowling a city alley.

His gaze found hers, night-dark eyes unblinking, and

so direct that any fiction she might have entertained that he had just wandered in casually off the street died.

Heads turned as he angled around a cluster of tables. The steady hum of conversation dropped away, so that he walked in a spreading pool of silence.

A group of women in the next booth, regulars who Anna knew were hookers working out of the bar, stopped their heated debate over the love-life of one of their friends. They were dressed in tight jeans and even tighter low-cut tops, with jackets pulled capelike over their shoulders for warmth.

"Is that for real?" one demanded. "Nita, how many beers have I had?"

"Not enough if you're still thinking of going home with that jackass you were eyeing before," came the dry answer.

"He don't have to pay," another one murmured.

The first woman who had spoken sighed. "Speak for yourself. I was thinking of paying him."

Anna jerked her gaze back to the booth she was supposed to be clearing. Blade had said he would check on her *tonight,* at her flat. She tried to isolate one believable reason for him to come looking for her today. There wasn't one.

Abruptly, she swung on her heel, abandoning the table and the tray as she began threading her way through the tables, heading away from Blade toward a side door that led to the rest rooms. There was a small storeroom next to the Ladies that was generally unlocked, as it had nothing in it that anyone would want to steal—not even the patrons of Joe's. It was usually crammed with mops and buckets and cleaning materials, but it had the added convenience of a bolted door that opened onto the dusty service entrance in back.

She quickened her step, her mind automatically putting together a strategy. If she could just get outside to the car park, there were any number of places she could hide. When she was sure Blade was gone, she could come back and claim her briefcase, which was stored in a staff locker. If she had to leave Joe's early and forfeit her money, then so be it.

The flat of her palm connected with the swing door. She was into the hallway, her heart pumping wildly, head faintly dizzy at the fast movement. Her hand closed around the door handle to the storeroom. For a crazy moment she thought it was locked, but then the stiff handle gave way. She stepped inside and gently closed the door behind her.

It was pitch-black. She didn't dare turn on a light in case he saw it and decided to check this room before the Ladies.

She heard the creak of the swing door as she picked her way gingerly forward, and her heart accelerated on another spurt of adrenalin. Her shin connected with a box, she gasped, shuffling sideways. The back of her hand brushed against a stack of what felt like broom handles. One more step and the door should be right in front of her. Her fingers encountered the heavy door, then searched for and found the cold metal of the bolt. She fumbled, easing the bolt back, then pulled the door inward.

Wind blasted into the room, thrusting the door back against her, almost knocking her off balance. A sound had her turning in time to see the widening arc of light as the other door swung open; then she was outside in the alley, damp wind cold around her legs, flattening her black skirt against her thighs and tugging hair loose from its knot so strands whipped around her face.

Anna heard her name, risked a glance over her shoulder, and saw him burst through the door. His black gaze seared into hers, and panic exploded through her. She knew Blade wouldn't hurt her physically, but she was too much on edge, too *hunted,* to respond in a rational way. She rounded the corner and broke into a run, her breath shoving hard into her lungs.

She had only gone two steps when his hand fastened on her arm. Instinctively, she jerked to free herself, and when that didn't work, she lashed out, her elbow driving back to connect with his stomach. He grunted as she pivoted to strike out with one foot, at the same time still desperately wrenching at his hold. But he was too strong, shifting every time she tried to hurt him, so that her blows glanced harmlessly off his body. Instead of breaking free, she found herself pressed face first against the unyielding surface of a concrete block wall, his muscled arm snaking around her waist, cradling her against the impact as his heavy weight pinned her.

Her heart was pounding, her breath coming in harsh pants. For a dizzying moment, she was paralysed by the blinding speed with which he'd moved, the easy way he'd handled her; then the intimacy of his hold registered. His arm was locked around her, his elbow snug against her hip, his hand splayed over her stomach and rib cage. The hold was at once confining and protective, and all he had to do was move his hand up an infinitesimal amount and he would be cupping her breast.

She could feel the steady rise and fall of his chest

against her back. In contrast to the damp chill of the wall, waves of heat rolled off him, penetrating her clothes so that her skin grew instantly damp. One big hand was planted beside her head. Without moving, she could see the strong sweep of his jaw, the softer curve of his lips, feel the weight of his gaze, as if he was willing her to look at him.

His hot breath stirred in her hair, and a small shiver swept up her spine. She could also feel something else stirring.

Anna drew a shallow breath, then another, and still he didn't move or let up on the pressure. Their pose suddenly struck her as blatantly sexual. When he had spun her around, she had automatically splayed her legs for balance. His arm had both cushioned her from the impact and tilted her torso so that she was angled in tight against his hips. Now the firm bulge of his arousal was lodged in the soft cleft of her bottom, and she was starkly aware of how flimsy a barrier cloth was. Added to that, her skirt was caught between them, rucked up high enough that she could feel cold air circulating around her inner thighs.

The hand beside her head curled into a fist, and she swallowed, her heart pounding almost as hard as it had when she had realised he would catch her. Abruptly, the warmth from his body and her own reached some kind of flash point, and a wave of smothering heat rolled through her, making her breasts prickle and swell, and a heavy ache flower low in her belly. Perspiration dewed her skin, so that she felt feverishly hot where her body was held tight against his and chilled where the cold pressure of the wind evaporated moisture from her skin.

"If I let you go, will you promise not to run?"

The soft rumble beside her ear made her jump. Instantly, she forced herself to stillness, startled by the giddy pleasure of being so close to Blade. The painful flood of confused yearning she'd felt last night washed over her again, and she pressed her cheek against the cold, gritty wall to stifle the mindless need to relax into his hold.

Once again, confusion rocked her. He was a stranger, and she was violently attracted to him. She didn't understand or trust any of what she was feeling. "I won't run."

He let her go slowly, as if he thought she might make a dash for the car park despite her promise. The thought passed through her mind, but she discarded it immediately. He would be on her before she could take more than a step. Smoothing her palms down her hips to straighten her rumpled skirt, she turned to face him.

His jaw was set, and a faint flush rode his cheekbones, giving the illusion that his dark eyes glittered with heat. He was furious and didn't care that she knew it. It was then that Anna noticed the earring. The small red jewel glowed against his lobe, catching the murky light like a drop of ancient warrior's blood. The earring was exotic, barbaric, like him, and it set the seal on his prowling restlessness. He could have been a pirate, a mercenary knight. There was a sense of enduring timelessness about him; if he were transported back several hundred years, he would fit right in.

His dark brows jerked together. "Are you going to tell me why you ran?"

Blade's irritable demand burned away the startling vulnerability he'd made her feel when he'd pushed her up against that wall. The plain truth was that she hadn't wanted to run, even though he had pinned her like a criminal, not bothering with social niceties like keeping his sexual arousal to himself. "Right after you tell me why you grabbed me," she snapped.

For a split second, he looked frankly incredulous that she'd bitten back; then amusement lightened the annoyance in his eyes. His gaze briefly dropped to her mouth. "Guess," he said flatly.

"No." Anna shook her head, rejecting the whole idea of a man like Blade being attracted to her, even though she had felt the reality of it.

She was slim, she had nice eyes and she had a mouth that men seemed to like. Big deal. She was also intelligent and very well-educated, although he couldn't know that. The only thing he really knew about her was that she was a waitress. She shouldn't even register on his personal scale.

"I can do a lot of things," he murmured, "but I can't fake sexual arousal."

She shook her head. "You don't want me." *You don't want what's following me.*

He looked impatient now, as if he weren't used to women arguing with him. His hand lifted, and for a disconcerting moment she thought he might reach out and touch her again. She braced herself for that disconcerting tingle, but instead, he appeared to take a mental step back.

"Okay," he said neutrally, "let's go back to the first question. Why did you run?"

Anna briefly considered telling him exactly what he could do with his question. She just as quickly abandoned the idea. His jaw was set, his gaze cop-cool and remote. She realised how big a mistake she had made in giving in to panic and running. It would have been smarter to have stood and faced him, preserving a polite distance. Running had incited all of his predatory instincts. "You scared me."

He frowned. "I told you I was going to check on you."

She edged away from him a half step. To her frustration, he followed her. "I didn't tell you where I worked. How did you find me?"

He glanced at her sweatshirt. "If it's such a big secret, you shouldn't wear the company uniform."

Anna fought off a hard jolt of pure panic. If Blade had found her this easily, then so could the man who had lain in wait for her last night. Had he seen her sweatshirt? She'd worn her raincoat most of the time, because it had been a showery day. He wouldn't have seen it when he attacked her, because it had been dark, and she knew her coat had been buttoned against the drizzle, but if he had been following her for several hours...

"You remind me of someone," he said, studying her with his head cocked to one side. "Around the eyes."

Anna stared at him in blank dismay, her heart once more pounding too hard and too fast. "No."

"Easy," he muttered, his voice low, the soothing tone all-too-familiar.

"I'm not a horse!" She glared at him, exasperated at his attempts to soothe her, and abruptly tired of the paranoia the last twenty-four hours had forced on her.

The flare of temper felt good. It was more natural for Anna to fight than run, and the temptation to challenge him with her suspicions instead of meekly retreating was almost too much. Taking a deep breath, she carefully blanked her expression and almost, but not quite, met his gaze. The trick was to imagine that a frosted panel of glass interrupted her line of sight so that even though she looked directly at his eyes, she never quite connected. "If you'll excuse me," she said coolly, stepping sideways again. "I need to get back to work."

"Dammit!" he roared. "Stop trying to run away!" Incredibly, he planted his hand on the wall, blocking her. "I'm sorry I had to grab you, but you shouldn't have run. I'm not going to attack you. I came to see how you are."

Anna's chin jerked up a notch at the way he was looming over her, as dark and bad-tempered as the storm clouds hovering overhead. Her own temper was on the point of exploding, and she was distantly amazed at her loss of control. She had kept her temper in any number of aggravating situations, from bar brawls to restaurant managers who thought they were God's gift to poor little waitresses. Five minutes with Blade Lombard and they were brawling and yelling.

"My head is a little achey," she retorted, "but otherwise, I'm one hundred percent, absolutely fine."

To her relief, he removed his hand and shifted back. His brooding gaze settled on her forehead. The lump had gone down, thanks to multiple applications of ice. This morning she had used make-up to mask most of the discolouration and the slight graze she'd sustained, but it was still obvious she'd hurt herself.

"You shouldn't be working."

Anna almost rolled her eyes at his simplistic view

of life. "Maybe not, but I need the money, and the only way to get it is to work."

Automatically, she checked that the knot in her hair was still tight. Strands were flying around her face, but she couldn't do much about that until she got to a mirror. Not that she needed to bother. Most of the patrons of Joe's were only interested in their food and beer. Godzilla could serve them, and they probably wouldn't notice.

"I need to talk to you. Take a break." The words were softly spoken but laced with command.

Anna eyed Blade with dazed disbelief. He actually expected her to obey his order. "I've had my break."

She could almost see his mind sliding over options, assessing, changing tack. If her head hadn't felt so fragile, she would have shaken it, except his presence wasn't funny. She still had to worry about why he had come after her and what that comment about her reminding him of someone meant. The two things just didn't go together. If he was hunting her as Henry was, he would know who she was, know that she resembled her mother in appearance. His perplexity over who she reminded him of had been real.

And just like that, she was struck with the clear certainty that he *didn't* know who she was. He wasn't hunting her. His presence in Ambrose Park, while mystifying, wasn't a threat to her. Her relief was in itself subtly alarming. She had wanted to trust him all along, and now she knew she could. Her instincts hadn't been wrong.

Which meant he had come after her because he was attracted to her.

Abruptly, she was swamped by a sense of loss. She

had never been so attracted to a man, never *wanted* like this, and it couldn't happen. She had to leave.

"What is it?" he murmured, moving closer.

A growl of thunder presaged the squall rolling in off the Pacific. On cue, big droplets of rain began pounding into the asphalt, and a cold gust of wind sent a scattering of rain under the partial shelter of the eaves.

Automatically, Blade shifted to shield her from the worst of it, his hand settling at the small of her back as he urged her back the way they had come. Numbly, Anna endured the burning warmth that flowed from the palm of his hand, desperately trying to analyse what it was that made her so acutely sensitive to him. He was only touching her out of courtesy, acting on the same instincts that had seen him help her out of her coat last night, but it didn't seem to matter—he touched her, and she reacted.

She found herself herded into the small storeroom. The rain was steady now, almost torrential in its intensity, making the close darkness of the cluttered room seem oddly intimate, although the partially open door into the corridor meant it wasn't completely dark. He had to let go of her once they were inside, because the path between the boxes of supplies and ranks of mops and brooms meant there wasn't enough space to walk abreast, but once they were out, his hand resettled against her back, heavy and warm, as he pushed open the swing door into the restaurant.

He wasn't touching her skin, and she could easily have moved away from him if she'd wanted, but even so, the pressure of his hand continued to unsettle her. He didn't need to touch her now, and with a flash of insight she saw his gesture for what it was: a possessive, territorial act by a dominant male. He was marking her as his.

The idea that he would want to do such a thing astounded Anna. Her knowledge of men was impressive and her opinion of them poor. She could write an encyclopaedia on how to avoid predatory men, the list of subtle and unsubtle nuances of body language that men construed as a come-on. But she knew very little about the rituals of courtship. All her adult life, she had carefully controlled relationships, keeping people at arm's length as a protective measure against the crippling hurt of loss. It had been a knee-jerk reaction for so long that she hadn't questioned it. She'd always had to move on, always been conscious that she mustn't draw anyone else into danger with her.

Blade's grip remained firm as he strolled with her back to where she'd left her tray. He seemed oblivious to the interest they were causing, but Anna wasn't. She could feel the weight of the attention, the speculation. She felt escorted. She felt *owned*.

She had to wonder if, like Alice, she had fallen down a rabbit hole into an alternate universe. Outside, Blade had deliberately let her know he wanted her. Pushing her up against that wall hadn't been intentional—she was the one who had set that course in motion by running—but once he'd had her there, he had used the opportunity. He had wanted her to feel his arousal.

When they reached the tray she'd abandoned, instead of leaving as she expected him to, Blade slid into the banquette she'd just finished cleaning.

Anna met his gaze, aware that everything she was feeling was written on her face, along with a healthy dose of panic, but she didn't care. He looked comfortably ensconced, as if settling in for a long stay. All she wanted was for him to leave before he made things worse. "I can't stop and talk with you. I have to work."

He shrugged. "Then I'll wait for your shift to finish."

"The shift finishes at five. That's two hours away."

"I'll have coffee while I wait."

He was going to wait for her! She felt as stunned as the time she'd been hit by a car: disbelieving, with all the wind knocked out of her. It seemed that whatever way she turned, Blade was there, cutting her off. She was beginning to feel like a mare being systematically driven and cornered by a stallion. "You won't like the coffee here," she said flatly.

He shrugged, his gaze intent beneath outrageously long lashes. "I'll have it anyway."

Clumsily, she scribbled his order on her pad, and then picked up her tray. When she came back with the coffee, he didn't try to detain her, for which she was grateful, but that didn't alter her awareness of him. He wasn't trying to be subtle about what he was doing; he *wanted* her to be aware of him, and his strategy was working.

Blade ignored the coffee as it steamed gently on the table. He was completely focused on Anna. She was wary of him, and he couldn't blame her. He had behaved like a caveman, but dammit, when she'd run from him, he'd been incensed, and when he had caught her against that wall, his fierce arousal had taken him by surprise. He had probably been as shocked as she was, but he hadn't wanted to back off. It had been all he could do not to grind himself against her, and he'd decided then and there that it had been as good a time as any to let her know the way things were between them.

She had tried to deny he wanted her.

He still felt incredulous at that. The only thing that had kept his temper in check was that she hadn't been able to hide her response to him. He'd felt the subtle changes in her body, seen the dazed blankness of desire in her eyes, even though she wasn't ready to admit to any of it yet.

Satisfaction eased some of his frustration as he watched Anna go about her job. She was pleasant and courteous, quiet and efficient. She walked with a graceful, no-nonsense stride that didn't quite succeed in being all business, courtesy of the feminine sway of her hips and the deliciously female shape of her bottom. The black skirt she was wearing ended just below mid-thigh, revealing legs that were slender, yet firmly muscled, with exquisite definition around the calves. They were the legs of an athlete, or someone who did a great deal of walking. He frowned at the thought of just how much walking Anna must do. She didn't own a car. Last night she had been attacked while out walking.

His gaze narrowed when he considered all that she was hiding from him. She had gone pale when she realised how easily he had tracked her down. He had a definite answer to one of his questions at least: she was on the run. Now all he had to do was find out from what, or whom, and then convince her to trust him enough that she would let him help her.

Of course, she could be running from the law—that would be something to check up on, although he would do the checking privately. If he found she was wanted by the police, he would make a decision about what to do when he found out how serious her crime was. Nothing about Anna suggested that she was a criminal, but appearances could be deceptive. She was feminine and soft, elegant and graceful, but her femininity hid a core of pure steel that kept stopping him in his tracks.

He hadn't got any further with finding out her real identity. She was prickly and defensive, and he was under no illusions that she would give up that information easily.

He would have to be careful with her. More careful than he had ever been with a woman. The steel had surfaced in her gaze a couple of times, and he suspected there would be occasions when they would fight like hell, but that only made him want her more. A woman who couldn't stand up for herself wouldn't interest him for long.

He went very still when he realised he was thinking in relationship terms, despite how little he knew about her. He examined the concept and felt a subtle relaxing of the tension inside him, a sense of having reached a decision.

He didn't know where any of this would take him, whether this was the beginning of a long-term relationship or just a short, fiery fling that, when the sex finally burned out, would be over, but he wanted to find out.

Anna had just finished clearing another table when a customer lifted his hand, catching her eye.

"Hey, darlin'. How 'bout my fries? I ordered them half an hour ago."

Anna eyed the three men sprawled in the adjacent booth, keeping her face carefully blank. They were young, muscled and tattooed, their gang affiliation emblazoned on their leather jackets, eyes jaded, flat with aggression. So far they'd been no trouble, but they had been drinking beer steadily as they ate. "I brought your fries."

"Then why am I still hungry?" he whined, holding his hand over his heart.

There was a burst of laughter, followed by some rough ribbing.

"If you're still hungry, I'll take another order."

"Don't be like that, sweet thing. I'm a man with...*appetites*. I was wondering what else might be on the menu."

Anna collected her tray. "We sell food and beer," she said coolly. "You want anything else, that's not my concern."

One of the hookers sauntered past, on her way back from the juke box. "Ignore him, honey," she said with a wink. "We'll take care of lover boy...if he minds his manners."

His hand snapped out, catching hold of Anna's wrist. "Maybe I don' wanna pay for it," he said softly. "Looked like you were serving up more than just coffee a few minutes ago."

Already off balance, Anna deliberately allowed her tray to tilt even further, so that a half-finished, iced soda tipped into his lap. He released her wrist to grab at the cup, leaping to his feet, swearing, as cold liquid soaked into the front of his jeans and ice-cubes scattered. "Why you—"

He lunged forward, trying to snag her wrist again, but Anna had already backed out of range, furious at herself for letting him grab hold of her in the first place.

His eyes narrowed in his flushed face as he flung the paper cup aside and started after her.

Anna heard one of the other waitresses yelling for Harry, the bouncer, who was occupied playing pool, but before Harry could intervene, Blade had cut in front of Anna, partially blocking her view.

"I wouldn't," he said.

His voice vibrated in a low, soft register, making all the hairs at the back of her neck stand on end.

The man froze, jaw dropping in an expression of ludicrous surprise. The whole restaurant grew silent, except for the snap of billiard balls connecting and the husky, background throb of a blues singer.

The young man's two friends stirred restlessly but didn't stand up to support their crony.

His gaze flicked to Anna, then slid away. "It's cool, man." His hands lifted, palms displayed, as he backed off. "Didn't realise she was yours. I was just havin' a little fun."

"Have it somewhere else."

To Anna's surprise, all three men backed off completely. Within seconds, they had vacated the booth, leaving nothing behind but the mess from their meal.

The doors swung shut behind the three men, and conversation returned to its normal level. Confrontation was part of the culture at Joe's, and on the scale of things, this one hadn't even been that interesting. No-one had thrown a punch; nothing had gotten broken.

Blade's attention immediately shifted to Anna, his expression still set in lines of cold ferocity. "Are you all right?"

For long seconds she couldn't answer; she was completely absorbed by this side of Blade, which she had instinctively known was there. He might be a businessman now, but beneath the mantle of expensive clothing, he was pure warrior.

"I'm okay. He didn't hurt me. I think he came off worse."

With a sigh, she set the tray down, snagged a cloth and went down on her haunches to clean up the spilled soda. She straightened up and tossed the soiled cloth on the tray, but then had to steady herself by gripping the edge of the table. She'd forgotten about her headache. Bending down had made her head swim.

Blade said something low and harsh beneath his breath. His hands closed on her upper arms, turning her to face him. "Don't you ever give up? You are *not* okay."

"It's just a headache. When I go out to the kitchen, I'll take an aspirin. Thanks for handling that guy for me."

His hands tightened on her arms. His head bent to hers, so that his face filled her vision, and she couldn't avoid his gaze locking with hers. His expression was intense, concerned. He wanted to help her, and his will battered her, wiped her mind clean of everything but him. For the first time in her life outside of those tormenting, insubstantial dreams, she shivered under the mesmerising need to yield to the fierce, male demand that burned in his dark eyes. He wanted to care for her, protect her. He was seducing her with a look, and she was losing the battle fast.

"Anna..." He paused, and she felt the sharpness of his frustration. "Dammit," he muttered. "I don't want you working here."

Anna blinked, utterly astounded. *He* didn't want her working here? "I have to finish my shift."

"Otherwise you don't get paid."

She stiffened. He knew. Somehow he knew that she was working illegally. The only way he could have found that out was if he had made inquiries. She swallowed her alarm, carefully blanking her expression. "That's right. If I don't finish my shift, I walk out of here with nothing."

"All right," he said slowly, as if he was making a major concession. "We'll do this your way, but I'm making sure you get home safely. What time does your shift finish?"

Anna repeated the time. He stared into her eyes for so long Anna thought he would challenge what she'd just told him. His perception was acute, the calm determination in his expression about as giving as tempered steel. She could feel his frustration at being thwarted simmering just beneath the surface, feel the control he exerted to keep it in check.

His gaze shifted to her mouth, but he didn't attempt to get any closer; the look was enough, hooded, weighted with an intent that made her shiver inside. He hadn't done anything so crude as kiss her in front of the interested audience in the restaurant. He hadn't needed to—that look had accomplished just as much.

"I'll see you at five," he said, and left.

Chapter 5

Blade started the Jeep, put the vehicle in gear and eased out of his parking space.

His hand tightened on the wheel. He was sweating, shaking, rage still burning through him. He'd decided to leave before he gave in to the impulse to pick Anna up and simply carry her out of there. He hadn't liked seeing her tired and run off her feet. He'd liked it even less when that young tough had come on to her, then almost dug his own grave by threatening her.

His teeth ground together. The cat and mouse game of seduction was damn well over. In his family, women were loved and cherished, protected. No-one—no man—it seemed, cared enough to look after Anna.

But he did.

The thought settled and took root as he cruised to the exit and waited for a break in traffic. When he picked Anna up tonight he would lay his feelings on the line and tell her she wasn't going back to Joe's. He didn't care what the hell kind of fight they had over it, but he wouldn't let her back inside that sleazy joint. There had to be any number of places she could work, jobs that she would enjoy more than waitressing.

He would find her another job. With Lombards. Although she would probably throw that suggestion back in his face. A wry flicker of amusement eased some of his tension. Nothing about Anna suggested that she would willingly accept charity. There was a fundamental dignity and pride underlying everything she did—a bedrock of honesty at odds with the way she was living. He didn't know why she was working illegally or living under a false name, but he was suddenly certain that when he investigated her, he would find that if she had broken any laws at all, she hadn't done so willingly. If she was on the run, it had to be because someone wanted to hurt her.

As Blade drove out of the car park, a brown sedan drove in. The man exited and walked into Joe's, limping slightly. He took a seat, instantly noting the hookers prowling the lanes between the tables, and viewed the menu, although he wasn't hungry. A waitress took his order, and while he waited for the coffee, he casually noted each of the waitresses working the tables. When he found the one he was seeking, he unfolded the newspaper he had carried in with him and disappeared behind it. His coffee arrived, and he drank it, grimacing because it was so bad.

When he was finished, he used the rest room, then went out to his car—which was positioned to watch the staff entrance—and set himself to wait.

* * *

An hour before her shift was due to end, Anna left Joe's—for good. She had cash in her pocket, although not nearly as much as she should have had. The manager, Rafferty, had short-changed her, paying her for less than half the hours she'd worked. She had expected him to rip her off, and she hadn't been disappointed. Rafferty had pocketed the bulk of her wages, openly enjoying her surge of helpless rage when he'd slipped the notes into his wallet.

She *needed* that money. But there had been nothing she could do, no protest she could make, and she wouldn't give him the satisfaction of pleading. The money she had would have to do until she could find a new job. Her carefully hoarded reserve of cash would get her through a couple of weeks, even a month, if she was careful.

Automatically, she studied cars and people as she walked toward the bus stop, but it was difficult to concentrate on who might or might not be wanting to kill her when the traffic and pedestrians looked so ordinary, and when the events of the past twenty-four hours had left her feeling alternately shattered and numb.

It had rained again just minutes before, but now the wind had dropped away and the sun was shining, warmth and light bathing everything in a hazy brilliance. Steam rose in wisps off the warming surface of the road. There were people strolling in open-necked shirts, coats slung over their arms, but she couldn't feel warm.

She had changed out of her waitressing uniform into jeans and a sweater before leaving, but even so, she huddled into her coat as she walked, one hand balled tight and shoved deep into a pocket for warmth, the fingers of her other hand locked around the handle of her briefcase, stiff with cold.

The cold came from somewhere deep inside her, like the chill of a fever or the onset of shock. She had felt it often enough to know she would have difficulty getting warm, no matter how many clothes she wore.

She came to a halt at the bus stop as the bus hove into view.

She'd made a start at stopping Henry's legal machinations yesterday and failed, but she wouldn't make that mistake twice. This time she would research her options thoroughly before exposing herself. What she was about to do both frightened and energised her. She felt as if she'd been caught and tossed up on the leading edge of a strong storm wind and was still tumbling wildly, but she had been running for so long, it felt good to finally turn and fight.

Once she established her identity and set the legal wheels in motion, she would have access to her own money. The dilemma of finding a job would cease to exist, although the thought of having money again hardly registered. She had spent the first twenty years of her life with access to a great deal of wealth, but it was hard now to imagine anything but scrimping and saving.

With a dawning sense of shock, she realised how restricted and closed her life had become. For nearly seven years she hadn't so much lived as survived. The stretch of time, of *years,* suddenly staggered her, so that she swayed where she was standing and had to reach out to the bus stop sign for support.

She had lost the best years of her life, years when

she should have been dating, falling in love, making a career for herself, maybe even getting married and starting a family. She was almost twenty-seven now, and she had less than nothing. She was alone.

Blade's face swam before her—his expression sharply male, black eyes not cool, but fierce with concern and something else that even now made her chest tighten against a pang of desolation. Tenderness.

She had given Blade the usual time for her shift to finish, omitting to tell him that today she had arranged to leave early. She had felt like she was betraying him—*she had felt like she was betraying herself*—but her decision had been made last night. No matter how violently she was drawn to Blade, no matter how tempted she was to lean on him and let him help solve her problems, she refused to drag him into danger with her.

The thought that Henry might harm Blade in some way sent a hot rush of fury through her. She wouldn't allow it, just as she wouldn't allow Henry to hurt her any longer.

The bus wheezed to a halt. The doors swished open, and automatically, she climbed on board, pulled her ticket from her pocket to be clipped, found an empty seat and sat down. She barely noticed any of the other passengers or the jerky stop-and-go rhythm of the bus as it wound slowly along its regular route. All her attention was focused inward.

For years she had blocked off her feelings, refused to feel, afraid of losing, because she had already lost so much. She had protected herself like a turtle pulling into its shell. She had survived by staying remote, by not loving anyone. Sometimes the cold crept so deep, she wondered if she would ever be warm again.

She was stretched so thin, close to the breaking point, and Blade had sensed it and ruthlessly homed in on her weakness, effortlessly smashing through her barriers. All it had taken was a touch, a word—that bone melting look—and she had been ready to give in, her awareness of him shattering her reserve.

He wanted her. She acknowledged that; but she also knew that if she let him any further into her life it would be a disaster. The danger aside, he would take everything; he would make her fall in love with him.

She was already half-way there, enthralled by his steely, uncompromising strength, those glimpses of humor and tenderness, the hot burn of sensuality, and the fierce purity of his will. She had never met anyone who burned so brightly; the essence of who and what he was blazed, the wash of power battering sensitive nerve endings every time she got close.

She didn't have the strength to love Blade and lose him. She had already lost too much of herself.

But even so, keeping the truth from him, leaving him now, hurt.

Blade arrived at Joe's early, driven by a hunch.

He strolled through the tables to the counter, scanning the already crowded booths.

The waitress at the cash register frowned when he asked for Anna. "She left early. I'm not sure when exactly, but Jenna's working her tables now."

Blade worked to keep his temper in check. His ice-cool nerves in combat were a fact; his control in any number of infuriating situations was a given. He *never* lost his damn temper. Lately, he was losing it every five minutes. "Will anyone know when she left?"

"Sure. She would have collected her money from Rafferty at the end of her shift. You want to talk to Rafferty?" She smiled as if it were some kind of joke, and gestured at a door off to the side of the counter. "Go on through. His office is second on the right."

Rafferty started up from his chair at the sound of approaching footsteps, almost spilling his hip flask of whisky over the mass of papers in front of him. His office door flew open as he lunged at the toppling flask, jammed the cap on and shoved it in his desk drawer, his temper going ballistic because all his staff *knew* they had to knock first, then wait until he was good and ready.

He could tolerate his cramped office space and the fact that he didn't have a secretary. He could even tolerate some of the smart comments he got from the dumb-ass syndicate members who owned this flea-bitten restaurant, but anyone who walked in without knocking first, was out of here so fast they would still be spinning when they hit the street.

A shadow loomed over him. Rafferty's head jerked up, mouth opening to vent his spleen. His mouth stayed open. He sat down very slowly and very carefully.

He had expected the new idiot cook, who had more questions than brains, maybe even that snooty waitress who had looked down her nose at him as if she wouldn't touch him with a barge pole, no matter how hard up she was. And he knew for a fact how hard up she was—money-wise, anyway—he'd made sure of it…not that it had done him any good. Anna Johnson hadn't so much as twitched that tight little ass in his direction, no matter how much he'd hinted he would like a piece of it.

The man standing in front of him was dressed in the kind of casual clothes that most of the patrons at Joe's wore: jeans, T-shirt, a leather jacket, long, black hair tied back in a ponytail, but that was where the similarity ended. He was big, broad-shouldered, all hard muscle and sharp intellect. There was a quality of stillness to the stranger, a waiting silence, that was subtly threatening, like a big cat in the moments before it sprang on some hapless, puny creature that had been singled out as a tasty snack. His eyes were spooky, glittering like black ice. Rafferty planted his backside further back in his chair. He didn't know what the stranger wanted, but he was certain he wasn't going to like it. "If you're looking for the bar," he said shortly, "you took a wrong turn."

"I know where the bar is," the stranger answered mildly. "I'm looking for Anna Johnson."

Rafferty jerked. Hot colour flooded his cheeks, and his heart pounded, so that for a panicky moment he had trouble breathing. "Anna Johnson." He tried to look perplexed. "Sorry, I don't know anyone by that name."

The stranger gently closed the door behind him and advanced further into the room, braced both hands on the desk and leaned forward, close enough that Rafferty couldn't miss the cold warning in his eyes. The deliberation of his movements made Rafferty break out in a sweat. He had visions of being worked over, of being beaten to a pulp, his body left sprawled across his desk for his useless staff to find.

"She worked here this afternoon," the man said softly. "She served me coffee."

Rafferty pressed down harder with his backside, so that his chair scooted back a bare inch, clanging against a filing cabinet. "If she worked here, I would know about it. I can't help you."

"I'll just bet you can, if you try real hard."

Blade watched Rafferty narrowly. His fingers twitched. He had to restrain himself from reaching across the desk and gripping the man's too-tight collar. If he got that close to Rafferty's neck, he would be tempted to choke him. The man looked like he ate too many of Joe's special double-beef burgers and fries, and his rat's nest of an office stank of whisky. Anna worked for Rafferty, and he was willing to bet that he ruthlessly ripped her off every chance he got. "Did she leave a forwarding address?"

There was a strained silence, broken only by the heavy wheeze of Rafferty's breath, and Blade wondered if he was going to expire from a heart attack right in front of him.

Rafferty reached for a handkerchief and blotted the sweat sheening his forehead. "You don't look like you work for the Inland Revenue department," he muttered.

"It must be your lucky day," Blade said with deadly calm, deciding that if Rafferty did keel over, he would probably dial emergency services, but he wouldn't be the one administering the kiss of life. "The name's Lombard. Blade Lombard."

The man's eyes almost popped from his head in startled recognition. He mopped his face again. "Anna quit this afternoon. She didn't leave a forwarding address."

"Did you pay her before she left?"

Rafferty flushed. "She got her money!"

Blade eyed Rafferty with disgust; he was lying. "For your sake," he said softly, "you better hope you paid her every cent she ever earned here, because otherwise, you will answer to me. Do you understand? When did she leave?"

Rafferty paled. "About half an hour ago."

Blade swore softly, spun on his heel and strode out of the seedy little office, his mind working with cold precision as he left the restaurant. He would deal with Rafferty later; right now he had a more important goal. Anna hadn't just left early, she had quit.

His jaw tightened. He'd had a hunch, and he'd been right. She'd run out on him.

As he swung behind the wheel of the Jeep and peeled out of the car park, he had another hunch, and this one didn't please him any more than the first one had. He wouldn't find her at her flat, either. She wasn't just running out on him, she was running, period.

He was going to be too late.

Anna unlocked the door to her flat and stepped inside.

With hurried movements, she packed a few fresh items from the fridge and pantry into a plastic carry bag, then placed it beside her bulging pack and briefcase. She had already cleaned and wiped everything down, the only thing left for her to do was to slip the key to the apartment in an envelope, along with a brief note, and address it to the landlord. She would post the letter on the way to the bus stop.

She was almost ready to leave, and now that the moment had come, she felt a fierce resentment that once again she was being pushed out of her home. She was only renting, but that had never stopped her from thinking of whatever accommodation she had as home. She had been here for several months, and in that time she'd given the walls a fresh coat of paint, and carefully selected and restored the dining table and chair. She'd unearthed the rug at a garage sale, then spent days beating it to get the dust out and reveal the subtle golds and blues beneath. Her collection of plants had all been grown from cuttings people had given her.

On a material scale, what she had might not be much, but it was *hers*.

A knock at the door made her start.

A soft, deep voice called out, "Anna, it's Tony."

Relief eased the tension knotting her stomach as she unlocked the door and let her neighbour in. She'd slipped a note under Tony's door before she'd left for work, asking him to call in when she got home, but for a heart-pounding moment she had thought it was Blade.

Tony Fa'alau's smile was gentle, but his liquid brown gaze sharpened when he noted the bruise on her forehead. "Who hurt you?" he demanded.

"I hurt myself, walking home last night." She lifted her shoulders, trying for a dismissive shrug. "It was raining. I slipped and banged my head."

Tony's expression was both disbelieving and disapproving. He didn't like it that she walked at night alone, and that she had no man to care for her. Anna had usually countered his argument by replying that he had no woman to care for him. Not that the argument worked. Tony Fa'alau was as stubborn in his own way as she was.

"You've got trouble."

"I've got trouble," she agreed, forcing a wry smile, because the last thing she wanted to do was upset Tony any further. "I'm moving today. I thought you or your family might like the pick of the furniture, or anything else here that you want."

Tony ignored the room, the furniture she'd offered him. Despite the grey streaks in his dark hair and the war wound that had permanently damaged one leg and kept him from full-time work, he was lean and vital, very much the head of his large, boisterous family. He lived alone, on a disability pension, but he kept himself busy helping his son, Mike, with the video parlour down the road. "If you've got trouble, we'll help you."

Anna's throat closed up at the simple declaration. Tony might be a widower, but he had four strapping sons, a parcel of gorgeous daughters-in-law and a large number of grandchildren. With that simple phrase, he had effectively offered her protection, but she couldn't accept it, because she wouldn't endanger either him or his family. "Thanks for the offer," she said quietly, "but I have to leave. I've notified the landlord. He's already arranged to put someone new in here." She took the spare key off the hook beside the door and pressed it into his hand before he could argue. "I'll leave this key with you, so you can take your time getting what you want."

Tony's hand closed over the key. "We won't take your things," he said stubbornly. "I'll get Mike to

store them for you until you can come back for them.
If you need help, call Mike at the parlour and he'll get
word to me.''

Tony made her promise to keep in touch and insisted
she write the number down, then watched like a hawk
as she put the slip of paper in her briefcase.

Minutes later, she'd done the final check of the flat.
Tony had retreated, giving her privacy, for which she
was grateful, because tears welled as she hefted the
pack on her back and slipped her arms through the
coarse canvas loops. She took a moment to adjust to
the weight and the balance of the load, shivering as the
cold inside her intensified. Then she bent to pick up
the plastic bag, her briefcase and the envelope for the
landlord, before pulling the door closed behind her.

A short time later Anna boarded the bus, settled in
her seat and stared out the window as the bus laboured
past her flat. With a start, she recognised Blade's Jeep
pulled over by the apartment block.

He had come after her.

Her stomach flipped queerly, and she forgot the cold,
forgot her tiredness, the tender ache of bruises and the
awkward bulk of her possessions pressing against her
on the seat. She craned, watching as Blade swung from
the cab, his expression grim, as if he already knew
she'd gone. A pang of loss struck through her, so intense she had to clench her jaw against the urge to howl
like a baby.

Why she should feel this way, she didn't know. It
was crazy; it was insane. She'd met Blade exactly three
times in her life—and one of those times had been
more than twenty years ago, when she had been a child.

They were no more than bare acquaintances pushed together by uncanny circumstance. Nothing more.

So why did she feel even emptier now than she had when she'd walked out of her flat?

Blade lifted his hand to knock on Anna's door, but the breeze caught it, so that it swung open before his knuckles connected.

A tall, older man, his black hair streaked with grey, was in the kitchen, packing household items into a cardboard box.

"What do you think you're doing?" Blade demanded, as he stepped into the room. He did a quick sweep, noting that Anna's possessions were all still intact. "Where's Anna?"

"She's gone." The man's gaze was dark, measuring. "I'm packing her things up before the new tenant gets here."

"You're Tony? From the flat upstairs?"

Some of the man's wariness faded. He nodded.

Blade relaxed, but only fractionally. "She mentioned you. Where did she go?"

Tony's expression went as blank as stone worn smooth by water. "She didn't say." He shrugged. "Guess if she'd wanted you to know she would have told you."

Minutes later, Blade stood by the Jeep, controlling the urge to slam his fist on the bonnet. If he'd been just a little earlier, he would have caught her, but he hadn't been quick enough. Now he didn't have a clue where to start looking. He had let her slip through his fingers, and the thought made him feel belly-cold, the way he had a couple of times on operations when he'd known that things were about to go sour.

He didn't know what kind of trouble she was in, but he was suddenly sure it was the worst kind. She was running like a woman who feared for her life.

She needed him.

Dammit all, why hadn't she trusted him to help her?

Chapter 6

Anna walked into her new home, a bedsit in a boarding house that had seen better days. Judging by the faded, peeling wallpaper, the crudely constructed kitchen counter in one corner and the bare wooden floor, those better days were somewhere back at the dawn of time.

Dropping the bags and the pack on the dusty floor, she unrolled a strip of snowfoam she had used more often than she cared to remember, laid her sleeping bag out on it, and simply kicked off her shoes and crawled into the bag, too exhausted to do anything other than lie flat on her back.

But the cold soon had her turning awkwardly onto her side and curling into a foetal position in an attempt to get warm.

Leaving had been more traumatic than she had bargained for. Blade had come after her! Her heart swelled at the thought, bursting with a strange mixture of heady delight and utter misery.

He would be furious that she'd slipped away. She didn't imagine that many women turned him down, although she doubted he would think of her for long.

Her eyes flipped open at that blunt truth, and she stared at the bare window. The evening was blue and tender, glittering with the first stars, and richly, achingly beautiful, but that didn't stop loneliness from gathering and expanding inside her, taking her over until she couldn't feel anything but the cold burn of having no one. Fiercely, she shook off the dark mood.

Minutes ticked by. She yawned, her eyes closed. She was still cold, but she was tired, too, so that she eventually relaxed from her tight, huddled ball and fell headlong into a deep, exhausted sleep.

The dream unwound like a slow drift of silk.

Midnight silk. His hair. She felt the satiny texture of it in her hands; her fingers wound deep in the warm, tumbled strands as she held him close and strained toward his misty, insubstantial face, desperate to penetrate the haze, to break through the frustrating barrier of anonymity and press her mouth against his.

His large hands tenderly cupped her naked breasts, and the exquisitely sensitive flesh swelled and throbbed, as if straining to fill his rough palms. His thumbs stroked over her tightly beaded nipples, heat flashed through her, and a moan burst from deep in her belly.

A shudder coursed through his big frame, as if he'd felt the same wild surge. He clasped her waist, one brawny thigh shifting between hers, the brush of his sex shockingly hot against her hip. In that moment he bent, and that fierce, beautiful mouth closed over hers.

Her legs went wobbly with relief as she yielded to the pressure of his mouth, the plunging stroke of his tongue. Her hands closed on his shoulders for balance, fingers sinking into pliant muscle. He was very big, making her feel small and fragile in his grasp, his chest and shoulders heavily muscled and damp with sweat. The kiss was long and deep, the rhythm drugging. His arms tightened around her as they clung together, his need matching hers. The searing heat of his mouth made her whimper and stretch, arching against the satin-hot smoothness of his chest, pressing closer.

The feverish need to get closer, to deepen the kiss, was overwhelming. She would be lost, left drifting in darkness, without his mouth on hers. He warmed her, anchored her, shoved back the cold.

She shifted restlessly, and in response, he lifted her up high against him, so that her feet left the ground and she had to cling to him for support.

A low sound of approval vibrated from his chest, shivered against her lips; then the firm, possessive grasp of his hands pulled her down. His body settled on hers, heavy, hot, sleekly powerful. She arched into him, stretching her arms above her head in a movement that was instinctive with him, and filled with a pagan ritualistic need. His fingers entwined with hers, holding her stretched taut beneath him as he nuzzled her, his breath warm against her cheek, her throat. Densely muscled thighs gently pressed her legs wide, the movement almost unbearably familiar, followed by the searing heat as he settled himself boldly against her.

He stilled, holding her cradled beneath him, gleaming, broad, sleekly muscled, his hair a tangled midnight mane brushing her cheeks, shrouding them both in darkness. The breath caught in her throat at his utter stillness, and she felt the cold shadows encroaching once more, pouring over and around her, stealing away the heat of his body.

She arched, desperate for his touch, desperate for the wildness and tenderness, for the first heavy plunge of his loins. When he was buried deep inside her there were no shadows, no chance of the icy chill stealing her away. Her life was bounded by absolutes. She was his, and he belonged to her. He would allow nothing else, no one else, to harm her.

The only thing she had to fear was her terrible vulnerability to his every touch.

A hand grasped her chin, his long fingers strong, calloused, gentle but firm against the tender softness of her skin, as he forced her gaze to his. His mouth was full, damp, reddened with extreme arousal, and set in a grim line. His eyes were slitted, still burning with raw need, and now with something far colder, far more controlled. An alarm of a new kind had her tensing against his hold—the hot, aching pressure as he held himself firmly against her loins, on the very brink of penetration.

There was no mist now, no shadowy outline; the strong sweeping lines of his jaw, his cheekbones, were starkly delineated.

Her heart pounded so hard that for a moment she had difficulty breathing. *She knew him.* The conviction burst to life somewhere deep inside her that she had always known him.

The odd sense of inevitability faltered as reality intruded. The mantle of anonymity that had cloaked her dream lover had been ripped away, and a new fear struck through her. She lay spread and helpless, utterly vulnerable beneath the muscled body of the protector she had already given herself to countless times, in countless ways.

The man she had opened her heart, her body, her very soul to, was Blade Lombard.

Recognition flared in his eyes; they glittered with disbelief and cold fury, colder even than the icy shadows that even now wrapped their tendrils around her.

"You," he accused in a dark rumble.

Anna flinched at the enraged rejection on his hard, warrior's face, his physical recoil as he reared back on his knees, leaving her frozen with a hurt that numbed her.

He had seen her face—he had recognised her—and he hadn't wanted her, his displeasure cuttingly sharp.

A pulsing ache started somewhere in the centre of her chest, rippled outward, expanding until a thin, anguished sound broke from her mouth.

She jackknifed, reaching for him, fingers sliding through shadows because he had already gone, shimmering into darkness with the dream.

Her sleeping bag had peeled back from her shoulders, leaving her shivering in the icy stillness of the room. She was still fully dressed, her clothes twisted and rumpled, and she was both hot and cold. Her skin was dewed with perspiration, her breasts tight, throbbing. She was still breathless, quivering with the aftershock of intense desire. She could feel the moisture between her legs, the heavy ache, as if her body really had prepared itself to accept a lover.

Blade.

The moon shone through her window, momentarily dazzling her, bathing her in its pale glow. She stared blindly at the misshapen disc through the grimy glass, her breath condensing in the air, jaw locked against tears as she struggled to orient herself, to free herself from the mesmerizing power of the dream.

It hadn't been real.

Oh, God. She squeezed her eyes shut, fighting back the stark desolation that always followed the dreams. When next she opened her eyes she forced herself to pick out the dim details of the room; the outline of the sash-window, the roofline of the lumbering old Victorian house next door, the virtual twin of this one.

She had seen his face. And this time there had been nothing fuzzy or indistinct about him; it had been Blade. He had looked into her eyes and recognised her, and he hadn't wanted her. The depth of the betrayal was stunning.

Anna shoved hair back from her face and scrambled to free herself from the tangle of the sleeping bag. She stumbled, almost falling over her pack as she searched for the light-switch.

The room flooded with light. She stood, swaying, arms wrapped tight around her middle to ward off the chill.

"It didn't happen," she muttered huskily, instantly knowing her words were a barefaced lie, because *something* had happened.

The dream had been intimate, earthy, exquisite in its intensity, her feelings so real they still stirred through her in prickling tremors. She was deeply drawn to Blade. More, he fascinated her. The terrible strength of that fascination was in itself frightening, because she had never had a physical relationship with any man. She had been too busy trying to stay alive to allow anyone that close.

The erotic dreams were intensely private, and even though they disturbed her, she was aware that sometimes they were all that kept her sane. She had always assumed they were a powerful, vivid fantasy born of her overactive imagination, her hunger for human contact, for warmth and love, but now she forced herself to view the underlying truth of the dreams.

As a child she had fantasised about a mythical being, a knight, who could protect her from de Rocheford. Regardless of the years and her own efforts to dismiss that particular fantasy, it had stuck. The dreams were also about her natural female need to mate—a need she had ruthlessly set aside.

It had all been simple and straightforward…until Blade had pulled her from that ditch.

She considered the possibility that her mind had somehow put Blade's face on that of her dream lover's, but she didn't think so. As stark as that moment of recognition had been, she hadn't been surprised. Horrified, maybe, but not surprised.

Somehow, she wasn't sure how, she was psychically connected with Blade and had been for years.

There were clairvoyants and psychics in the Montague line. Her grandmother had been able to see auras. Anna's mother had claimed to be clairvoyant. Anna knew she had neither of those talents. She had assumed she had been relatively untouched by the witchy Montague genes and had been quite frankly relieved. The only thing she had ever laid reluctant claim to was a

certain empathic sensitivity to people. It wasn't anything she could explain, other than as some kind of
amplification of the instincts and awareness that everyone possesses to a greater or lesser degree. She wasn't
even sure what she *did* feel. The best way to describe
it was that she could feel the soul, the essence, of someone. She'd been maybe six or seven when she'd realised that the outside of Henry wasn't the same as the
inside. He'd had a secret. She hadn't known what it
was then, but she'd known enough to keep away from
him.

Maybe that was why de Rocheford had turned on
her so quickly after he had married her mother; he had
known she'd seen through him. He'd been afraid of
her. She'd sensed his fear like a discordance interrupt-
ing the cold flow of his anger, but "knowing" hadn't
helped her; she had never been able to convince anyone
that Henry wasn't what he appeared to be.

If Henry was cold, Blade burned. His essence battered at her like a hot wind, so powerful she wondered
that she hadn't recognised him immediately. Vitality
spilled from him like heat from a furnace, pouring
through her with every touch. She had been right as a
child when she'd decided that angel wings didn't fit
him, Blade was too aggressively male to ever be called
an angel.

No, he wasn't an angel. He was the secret friend she
had called out to, the knight she'd woven fantasies
around, the powerful lover who had haunted her
dreams.

Every touch should have told her who he was.

Now she had to wonder if he knew who *she* was.

* * *

Blade flung the twisted covers off his bed and stalked to the French doors, pushed them wide and stepped out onto the balcony. He was naked. Hot. Wildly aroused. Furious.

He had dreamed. His jaw locked on another violent surge of arousal. He braced his hands on the wet steel of the balcony railing and waited out the hot, raw intensity of the ache.

Anna Johnson.

He pushed away from the railing, shoving long fingers through his sweat-dampened hair as he prowled the length of the terrace.

Sweet Mother of God, this time the mysterious woman in his dream had had Anna's face.

He let his mind sift over the jolting shock of discovery. The moment of utter disbelief and rejection of something that just couldn't be.

But it *was,* he thought grimly. It was the only thing that made sense.

The certainty of the knowledge settled into his mind like the last missing piece to a puzzle that had frustrated him for years. He knew the arch of her throat, the delicate curve of her earlobes, the narrow span of her waist and the gentle fullness of her breasts, as intimately as he knew his own body.

It was her.

His eyes narrowed on the moon as it eased below the jagged line of city buildings, his hands knotting into fists as he fought the heavy fullness of his loins and waited for the icy drift of the breeze to work its cold magic.

He'd almost disgraced himself like a teenager. He'd gotten so hot his skin had felt like it was on fire, and he'd sweated so much the sheets had been soaked. His need was still so fierce he wanted to howl. Anna had been twisting beneath him, soft, exquisitely open, waiting....

Another wave of heat slammed through him, laced with a sharp sense of loss, and he briefly considered the cleansing pain of slamming his fist into a wall. Better yet, he should use his head. He had had Anna within his grasp, and he had let her get away.

The implications of the dreams, the visions, shuddered through him. If the hauntingly intense, erotic dreams were real, then so was every dangerous event he'd "witnessed."

He needed to find her. Now.

Blade strode inside and began jerking clothes on, burying his fear beneath the cold burn of anger that Anna was out there alone and in danger. The only lead he had was Anna's flat. He would search it. If he was lucky, he might find some clue as to where she had gone—a scribbled note, a telephone number. Something, anything.

He should have searched the damn flat while he was there earlier, instead of cruising the streets, scrutinising all the bus stops. He didn't know if he would find anything useful once he was inside, but he had to try.

He would find her. It was just a matter of time.

Blade parked the Jeep near the entrance of Finnegan Street and checked the clip on the Glock before slipping it into his shoulder holster. He shrugged into a black leather jacket and grabbed a pair of night-vision goggles from the passenger seat. He'd had enough of stumbling about in the dark the previous night. The goggles wouldn't be any use out on the street—the ambient light was too great—but the rear of the apartment block was pitch black, and he would need to reconnoitre the area before he risked breaking in.

It was black as hell's kettle as he stopped beneath the cover of a large, weeping shrub to fit the goggles. Immediately the backyard of the ratty apartment block sprang to ghostly life. A sagging tin shed, an old Volkswagen on blocks, more dirt than grass, a washing line stretched between two poles.

Blade took note of the properties bounding the building, and any fences or obstacles he would have to negotiate if he had to make a quick exit. There were no dogs, for which he was thankful. Dogs were hell on breaking and entering.

He was about to step up to Anna's window when he caught a faint movement. He stayed where he was, watching, disbelief changing to cold fury. The outline had been male. Maybe someone was simply turning the flat over, stealing whatever Anna had left behind, but he didn't think so. Anna had owned very little that anyone would want to steal, and whoever was in there was also wearing night-vision gear.

Minutes later the man exited the flat, the night vision gear no longer in evidence, a small duffel bag slung over one shoulder. Blade remained motionless beneath the dense cover of a tree, tracking the man's movements. ''Oh, yeah,'' he said softly. ''I see you now.''

The man wasn't tall, five-eight, maybe five-nine, and powerfully built, with a face that had seen a lot of action. He was dressed in dark clothing. His manner was calm, confident and professional.

Blade trailed him, watched the man stroll to a brown

sedan parked out on the road. Coldly, Blade considered his options, and dismissed the idea of following. By the time he got the Jeep turned around, his chances of locating the dark sedan would be minimal. He took note of the licence plate. As the car eased away from the kerb, he retrieved his cell phone from his pocket and made a call to an ex-SAS contact, Ray Cornell, who was now a police detective.

Ray didn't like being woken up, but, typically, he was instantly alert. "This isn't legal," he muttered, as he took the details of the licence plate.

"It'll be worth your while. I think you might want this guy."

Blade relayed his number and terminated the call. Minutes later, Ray rang back with a name. "Eric Seber. We want him," he confirmed tersely, "but we haven't been able to nail anything solid on him yet. He's an ex-cop, ex-mercenary, who's put himself on the market as a 'security consultant.'"

Blade stared at the space Seber's car had occupied, every muscle in his body tensing. "What do you want him for?"

"I can't tell you that."

Blade was silent.

Ray sighed. "Okay, I owe you one, Lombard. Word is that he's a hit man, that's all I can tell you—that, and to stay out of his way. He's got some heavy duty connections."

"How heavy duty?"

"If we knew that for sure, we'd have the bastard."

Blade ended the call and went up to the flat. The door was open. When he switched on the light, he saw that the place had been completely trashed. Not that there was much left to trash. The bed and table and chairs were missing, and so were all of Anna's clothes and personal possessions.

Potted plants had been strewn on the floor—the soil dumped in piles, the plants discarded with their roots exposed. An old vinyl couch had been gutted. The fridge and all the cupboards in the tiny kitchenette were open, the remaining items strewn over the floor and counter.

Blade didn't like the picture he was getting. The man had been too professional for simple vandalism. He'd been looking for something, and he had gone through the small flat with brutal, systematic efficiency.

He bent and picked up a cheerful calender. Flowers. He paged through it, checking for any handwritten notes, and found none. His mood got grimmer. Anna liked flowers.

He surveyed the damaged plants, the wilting petals ranging in colour from pale pinks and yellows to a cheerful neon orange, and rage dug itself a place in his gut, simmering there like a hot coal. His mother liked flowers. She collected them, babied them. She even talked to them. Bridget Lombard wasn't happy unless she had her fingers sunk deep into soil or was spending a fortune in some garden centre. If someone did this to her plants, she would cry—right before she declared war on the perpetrator.

Something about Anna reminded him of his mother. Not in looks; it was something else, a kind of luminous inner grace and dignity that permeated everything she did and almost seemed to glow through her skin. It was the sort of quality that made you stop and consider before you did anything at all that might possibly hurt her.

Setting the calender aside, Blade began collecting the plants, carefully packing them back into their pots with whatever soil he could gather up. When he was finished, he placed them in the back of the Jeep.

He made one more pass through the flat, searching for any pieces of discarded paper, but the mess the intruder had made aside, Anna had been frustratingly neat. Evidently she'd disposed of the rubbish before she had left or had someone do it for her. Her neighbour, maybe.

He knocked on the door of the flat above. There was no answer.

The games parlour just down the street was still open. Blade eyed it thoughtfully. After stashing the night vision goggles and the Glock in the Jeep, he headed for the parlour.

The place was barnlike in its immensity and even at this late hour was doing a busy trade, pulsating with bursts of light and sound. A tall, lithe man with the darkly handsome features of a Maori or a Pacific Islander rose from his kneeling position by a machine he had been tinkering with and strolled over.

"You looking for someone?" he demanded softly, his gaze watchful.

Blade eyed him with interest. The man was almost ruthlessly clean cut, his gaze direct, sharply intelligent, with a cool confidence Blade instantly recognised. He had seen that look in cops, but he was willing to bet that until very recently, this guy had been a soldier. "I'm looking for Tony."

"You a cop?" The man's intense gaze swept Blade,

added up his long hair, the leather jacket, the stud in his ear. "You don't look like a cop."

"I'm a friend of Anna's."

The man continued to eye him, not acknowledging his words or that he knew who Anna was. He turned his head slightly, not taking his gaze off Blade, and yelled, "Dad! Someone to see you."

Tony emerged from a back room, favouring one leg, a mechanical part in his hands.

The man's gaze remained locked with Blade's while he talked to his father. "You know this guy?"

"I've seen him."

"Says he's a friend of Anna's." His voice was flat, neutral. He was still reserving judgment.

Blade's assessment of him went up another several notches. He was protecting Anna.

Tony handed his son the machine part he was carrying. "That's fixed," he said laconically. "Damn cheap wiring." He switched his attention to Blade. "He came looking for Anna this afternoon, but she'd already left."

"You her man?" the son demanded softly.

Blade returned the challenging stare with one of his own. "Yeah," he said in a silky rumble. "I'm her man."

"Then how come she walked out on you?"

Blade smiled grimly. "She doesn't know I'm her man yet."

The silence following his pronouncement stretched taut, emphasised by the waves of tinny game music, the exultant whoop of a player, a shout of laughter.

Abruptly Tony chuckled. "Looks like Anna's finally

got herself someone, whether she wants him or not. It's all right, Mike, I can handle this.''

Mike nodded, still eyeing Blade with a searching reserve, as if he would like to question him further. Blade let him look his fill, understanding that Mike wanted his own reassurance, because if he were in the same position, he would do exactly the same. Finally, Mike nodded and strolled back to the machine he'd been repairing.

Blade turned, his gaze narrowing on Tony. ''Where is she?''

''Like I told you before, she didn't tell me where she was going.''

''Someone broke into her flat tonight. They trashed it.''

Blade saw the consternation on Tony's face and pushed his advantage. ''I need to find her. I saw the guy leaving her flat. He's a professional hit man. I need to find her before he does.''

Tony swore softly beneath his breath. ''I don't know where she went,'' he said, ''but I can tell you where we can start looking. Anna spends a lot of time in libraries. She's writing a book. If we check out the libraries, she'll turn up.''

Chapter 7

The next evening, the library was quiet, filled with the weighty hush of carefully turned pages, the low-level hum at the front desk as a steady stream of evening customers got their nightly fix of reading material, plus the occasional creak or scrape of a chair as reading tables were used and abandoned.

Anna chose another book from her pile of legal tomes and began checking the index for references on the whole grey area of declaring a missing person dead.

From what she could discover, Henry must have applied to hold an inquest into her ''death.'' He had obviously been instructed by the court to advertise his intention to have her declared dead in all the major newspapers. Without a body—and with doubt being cast on her ''death'' by a number of unsubstantiated reports from supposed eyewitnesses—there was no clear evidence that she was dead, just missing.

He had been forced to endure the maximum legal waiting period of seven years because of the doubt—and to allay suspicion. If he had tried to declare her dead immediately after her car had been found, half submerged, at the base of the cliff, there *would* have been suspicion, because she had approached the police just months before, after a so-called accident when she had been sideswiped by a car. Even if nothing could be proven, Henry's interest in her death would have been clear.

But Henry's need to legally establish her death was perfectly understandable and logical at this point. He had waited the allotted time, as the situation with his troublesome stepdaughter had dragged on. He had been managing Tarrant Holdings for years; it was rightfully his in all the ways that counted. The legal proceedings would barely cause a ripple in the business world.

She flicked open her briefcase and pulled out a folder of newspaper clippings, most of them yellowed with age. There were several that reported unconfirmed sightings of the Tarrant heiress, and they had succeeded in muddying Henry's legal waters even further. According to the guidelines for coroners she'd just read, any element of doubt would stay the proceedings. She would still need to prove her identity, but that was a separate issue. All she had to do was present herself at a police station, or at her solicitor's, and swear an affidavit that she was Anna Tarrant, and the proceedings to have her declared dead would be halted.

A wave of relief swept her. She would still have a fight on her hands, a battle to stay alive, but that she could handle.

* * *

Blade strode up the library steps, pausing to allow a stream of students loaded down with books through the door. Along with the help of the Fa'alau family and a security firm he'd hired, he'd had every library in the city staked out, and it had paid off.

He'd expected to have to wait several days for Anna to show up, but even so, the hours he had waited were too long. Impatience rode him hard, and he had to keep a rigid clamp on his temper.

His jaw tightened on a fresh surge of disbelief and outrage that she had run from him.

He had been spoiled when it came to women, he knew it, and he had enjoyed the attention. Maybe that was no excuse for the betrayal he felt, but dammit, he was used to women seeking him out, not running away. That the woman he had been dreaming about for half his life—the woman who had obsessed him for years—had walked away without a backward glance, as if he were no more than some casual acquaintance, drove him crazy.

Blade saw her as soon as he walked into the reading room—and she saw him.

Her eyes widened in horror—just the kind of effect he loved to have on the ladies. She jumped to her feet and began stuffing papers into her briefcase.

Incredulous fury filled Blade as he watched her slam the briefcase closed and dart behind a set of shelves. Even now, she was running from him.

It wasn't hard to catch her; whichever direction she ran, she couldn't get out unless she went past him to the main door. He caught her as she tried to dodge around another aisle of bookcases. His hand curved around her upper arm, stopping her short. He shuddered inside at that simple touch, his fingers tightening convulsively. She was wearing the same drab raincoat she'd had on the other night, but it didn't seem to matter; whatever special quality the lady had, whatever chemical attraction existed between them, she could be wearing a sack and she would still turn him on.

This time she didn't try to hit or kick him—he supposed he should be thankful for small mercies—instead she went very still.

Abruptly, she turned on him. "Leave me alone."

She jerked against his hold, making him feel like a villain. Blade let her go, and she stumbled back in her haste to be free of him. The briefcase she was holding clamped under one arm slipped and gaped open, spilling papers on the floor.

"Now look what you've done!" She shot him an accusing glare that *did* make him feel like a villain as she bent to retrieve them.

Blade went down on his haunches to help her. He picked up a handful of old, yellowed newspaper clippings.

She snatched them from his grasp. "How did you find me?"

Bemused, he watched the feverish speed of her hands as she stuffed papers into the case. "Tony said you hang out at libraries."

"Tony wouldn't tell anyone—"

Blade's eyes narrowed with annoyance. "He didn't tell *anyone*." He sucked in a breath, amazed to find that his heart was pounding and he actually felt nervous. "He told me where you were likely to be because he trusts me." *Unlike some people.*

Her expression said that Tony was the biggest fool

in this corner of the known universe. "How did you know I was in this library?"

"I had people watching all of them."

He saw the widening of her eyes as she absorbed the massive manpower he had utilised to find her, the fear that jerked through her and was just as quickly hidden. "Anna," he said, low and rough, "I wouldn't have done it if I didn't think you were in some kind of trouble. We've got to talk—"

She shook her head. "We've got nothing to talk about."

Nothing to talk about?

His breath sifted from between clenched teeth, and he fought the desire to grab her close and find out first-hand if her lush, pale mouth was as soft as it looked. She'd been invading his head for years, and she didn't want to talk about it?

He felt incredulous, he felt insane—and through it all he still wanted her. He should do it, kiss her—the hell with chivalry. He needed to kiss her, hold her. He needed to have her clinging to him. The compulsion to simply grab her was almost overwhelming.

She was all business as she shoved the last crumpled paper in the case. More papers fell out, and she sank to her knees and began the struggle to repack the case all over again. Blade was certain he saw the glitter of tears in her eyes, and something twisted deep inside him. He had pushed her too far, more concerned with his own ego, his male pride, than whatever demons she was fighting. She was crying, and it was his fault.

He gathered her hands in his. When she didn't resist, he stood, coaxing her up, his hands settling on her arms, rubbing, soothing. She didn't try to wrench free of his grasp or resist him in any way, and conversely, now he wanted her to fight.

After her frantic attempt to escape, she was unnaturally still, her eyes suspiciously bright, but remote, as if she wasn't quite meeting his gaze. "I thought that once I left, you would forget about me."

Her statement was curiously calm and reasoned after the way she'd tried to run, but Blade didn't miss the flash of vulnerability in her eyes. She had expected him to forget, but she hadn't wanted him to. Satisfaction eased some of his ferocious tension.

"I can't forget you," he said bluntly. And just in case she was still having difficulty grasping the concept, he added, "I want you." It was ground out between clenched teeth, low and harsh, but he couldn't be soft and gentle when he was burning up inside, when he'd been on edge for hours while he searched for her, wondering if he would be too late.

He wanted her. It was the truth, and he didn't like it.

He didn't understand the bond between them, and he hadn't asked for it; all he knew was that he had to have her, and there was no room for subtlety. He had to lay claim, now, to get her to trust him, to tell him what she was running from and let him help her.

The pupils of her eyes dilated wildly, black swamping silvery-grey until he thought she might faint, but she remained steady in his grasp. The only other physical betrayal was the quickness of her breathing.

Oh, yeah, he thought grimly, Blade Lombard, master of seduction. First he strikes horror into her fragile soul, then he comes on to her with about as much subtlety as a stag in rut. He now fully understood why his brother, Gray, had gone to pieces when he'd been courting Sam, the woman he had married. Gray would be rolling on the floor, roaring with laughter, if he ever found out about any of this.

Despite his bluntness, he could almost hear Anna's agile mind ticking over, searching for a loophole in what he'd just said. He had to wonder what had made her so suspicious of relationships and so utterly lacking in self-confidence. A woman who looked like Anna would have had plenty of men hitting on her regardless of the fact that she didn't seem to do one thing to try to attract them.

She shook her head, as if coming to a decision. "You should let me go, Blade."

Her voice was low, strained, and Blade couldn't help thinking there were a lot of other words, other phrases, he would like to hear that mouth shaping, but words weren't necessary. She wanted him. He saw it in her eyes, felt it deep and hard in his gut.

He lowered his lashes to veil the shock of raw desire that ran through him, the instant heaviness in his loins. She was so damn skittish, he didn't want to scare her any more than he already had. For some reason, she felt she had to push him away.

Before they made love, he would find out what the reason was and fix it, because once he had her in his bed, he didn't want any more secrets between them. He didn't want to go to sleep wondering if she would still be beside him when he woke up the next morning.

But now wasn't the time to push for more physical intimacy. He'd already gained far more than he had expected. If she needed time to accept his presence, his touch, then she could have it, but he wasn't backing off. And he wasn't letting her out of his sight, not with a hit man like Seber on her tail.

"Do you want me to let you go?" he asked, the question forced from him. He waited, every muscle clenched against her response.

For an endless moment her eyes were wide and blank and curiously lost. "No," she said huskily.

Relief poured through Blade, swiftly followed by elation, but he forced himself to release her and step slowly back. It wasn't what he wanted to do. He wanted to snatch her up and take her back to his place and spend the rest of the night in bed, making love. He wanted to have her naked beneath him and keep her there until she knew that was where she belonged. But if he wanted to gain her trust, he had to start somewhere. He had pushed her hard enough for now.

Anna swayed where she stood, bracing herself against the emotions that tumbled through her mind and rioted through her body. When Blade had asked her if she wanted him to let her go, he hadn't been talking about his physical hold on her arms. She hadn't been able to lie, but she had just agreed to...what?

He'd come after her, and he had found her, using all the considerable resources at his disposal. When his dark gaze had fastened on hers it had been sharp, predatory, and for an endless moment she had been unable to breathe, almost strangled by disbelief and her own longing. He was dressed in scuffed boots, a snug pair of faded jeans, a white T-shirt that clung to his broad chest and a supple black leather jacket. In the dull confines of the library he had looked big and dangerous and mouthwateringly gorgeous.

She hadn't thought about Henry or running for her

life. She had instantly known that the source of Blade's fury had been that she had run out on him. She had read his sexual intent and panicked, although she suspected sex was the wrong word to describe what Blade wanted. With him, the act would be elemental, powerful, and he would be wickedly good at it.

Heat burned deep inside her when she considered how she knew so much about Blade's sexual prowess. He would sweep her up, sweep her away, like the river that had almost taken her life when she was eleven. She would be lost. She knew it as surely as she knew Henry wanted her dead, but the temptation to take those few hours or days, to give herself over to the raw power of his lovemaking, the tender intensity of his touch, had smashed down every last defence. She'd had so little, taken so little, for herself. She had looked into Blade's eyes and quite simply been overwhelmed.

Blade stooped to pick up her case and a loose clipping that lay beneath it. She retrieved the clipping from between his fingers, barely restraining herself from snatching again, and stuffed it in her jeans pocket so he couldn't read any more than he already had.

She could feel his gaze like an actual weight on her skin, and her pulse kicked wildly.

"Have you eaten?"

She blinked, surprised by the innocuous question. She'd expected him to ask about the newspaper cutting or why she'd run from him. A hundred questions but that one. "No."

"Okay, I'll give Tony a ring, so he can call off the troops, and then we'll go and get some dinner."

Anna went very still inside. "Tony's been out looking for me, too?"

"He was worried about you, just like I was."

"I'm not used to people…worrying."

"Then you better get used to it—fast."

Her stomach clenched, distracting her from asking why Tony had been worried enough to go out searching.

Blade picked up her hand, laced her fingers with his in a slow, deliberate movement. His hand was large and darkly tanned, and it completely engulfed hers. It would be like that in bed, she thought. He was so big and broadly muscled; she would be helpless against him. Yet his hold was gentle, controlled, as if he was very aware of his strength and was careful not to hurt her.

He didn't try to pull her along to the door but waited patiently, watching her with a calm intensity. He wanted to mould her to his will, but he was asking…after a fashion. He looked so bad-tempered beneath it all, heat smouldering beneath all that steely control, that a wry smile tugged at the corner of her mouth, and she felt the subtle shift inside her caused by that brief moment of humour—the warm rush of emotion that rolled through her with the lazy power of an ocean swell, threatening to knock her off her feet. She felt the moment she fell in love.

Abruptly, the shimmering warmth changed to dizziness as the room began circling slowly around her.

"Don't faint on me now," Blade murmured right next to her ear. His arm was at her back, supporting her, easing her forward until her face was buried against his chest. She rested against him, drinking in his hot, male scent and wondering if she should tell him that this wasn't helping one little bit. How was she supposed to resist him, how on earth was she supposed to pull back from loving him, when he kept making her fall deeper and deeper?

His hand pressed the small of her back, urging her closer still. She felt his chin brush the top of her head.

"Tell me you're not fainting because I've just offered to buy you dinner." His voice was little more than a rumbling vibration against her ear.

"I'm not fainting because you offered to buy me dinner."

He eased her slightly away from him, his expression whimsical, searching. She felt his fingers at her wrist and realised he was taking her pulse.

"You need to eat."

"Not hamburgers."

Amusement tugged at his mouth. "Hell, no. Are you all right to walk, or should I carry you?"

He was serious. If she wanted, he would pick her up and carry her.

Anna shook her head in bemusement. "I can walk."

"Damn," he said softly. His smile turned into one of those mesmerising grins as he kept his arm around her and started toward the exit. "We won't go near a hamburger joint," he promised. "You can have anything you want. Pizza, sushi, Chinese. Anything. Just name it."

Happiness unfolded itself somewhere in the region of her heart and bubbled giddily through her veins. She should hold on to caution, tell him no, because the plain fact was that this man was dangerous to her. He was holding her close against his side as if she were something precious. They were going to eat dinner somewhere—she was hungry, *starved*—and she was drunk on the sheer delight of just being with him.

He took her to a small Italian restaurant with warm, sun-browned walls, tables covered in checkered cloths and decorated with candles stuck into Chianti bottles. There were plenty of customers wearing jeans and sweaters, so she didn't feel out of place.

They ate pasta and salad, and drank ice water. Blade didn't order any alcohol, and she didn't need it; her blood was literally fizzing through her veins.

He didn't question her any further, even though she could feel the weight of all he wanted to ask. For the moment he seemed content to tell her about his family, the new house he was building and the horse stud he had planned, the oil painting he was working on in his spare time, the casino that was being added on to the Lombard Hotel complex. She knew he was deliberately relaxing her, but she didn't care.

As they left the restaurant, he took her arm, the action was casual, but that wasn't how it felt. The first brush of his fingers sent a charge through her, followed by a wash of heat that made her shiver in reflex and her chest tighten on a startled intake of air.

His hand jerked back as if, this time, he had felt it, too.

He said something low and rough. His hands clasped her upper arms, and he turned her to face him beneath the light of a street lamp. This time the jolt was low level, more of a tingling hum. "Did you feel that?" he demanded. "Sometimes when I touch you, I feel something…extra. A heat."

Anna pulled free from his touch. "I don't know what it is."

"Has that ever happened to you with anyone else?"

"No."

His gaze was still almost chillingly speculative, and for a moment she was transfixed by the dawning suspicion that *he knew*—that somehow he knew about the dreams.

Heat and confusion tumbled through her, along with a deep unease. The dreams were intolerably private. That Blade could possibly be aware that they'd shared those primitive matings, that he'd used his mouth on her breasts, made love to her while she'd clung to him, while they'd clung together...

The restaurant door flipped open behind them on a wave of music and laughter. A young couple exited, glancing at them curiously.

Blade held out his hand, and after a moment she gave up on resistance and placed her hand in his. His clasp was firm but gentle as they walked to where the Jeep was parked, as if he was being very careful not to scare her, yet the warm pressure of his fingers was also disturbingly intimate. He had pushed until she had accepted his touch, reinforcing his right to touch her.

He helped her into the Jeep, then walked around and got in, but he didn't immediately start the engine. "Do you want me to take you home?"

His face was in shadow, but she could feel the intensity glittering in his half-closed eyes, knew that if she indicated she was willing, he would take her to wherever he lived and spend the night making love to her. The thought sent a shock of pleasure through her, so strong that she fumbled with the seat belt.

"I have to look for work tomorrow." It was no kind of answer, but she just couldn't bring herself to say either yes or no. The inevitability of what Blade wanted pulled at her like a powerful tide, and she was helpless against it, but she also feared it. For Anna, making love was inextricably entwined with commitment. She had never set out to be either prudish or calculating. That was simply the way she was. If she made love with Blade, she would want everything else that went with it. Marriage, family, the whole kit and caboodle, and she had no idea what he wanted from her. She was in love with Blade, but essentially, they were strangers.

"Are you married?"

Her head jerked up, eyes widening. *"No!"*

"Good," he murmured. "Because I'm going to kiss you."

Silence followed while he unclipped the belt she'd just fastened and let it slide back into its slot. The silence pooled and grew until she could feel it throbbing, pulsing in her throat, making it difficult to breathe.

He bent forward, cupping her nape, but instead of the kiss she expected, he nuzzled her neck, rubbing his jaw softly against her skin, sending hot shivers of anticipation through her. She could feel his lips at her throat, her jaw. The pleasure of the light caresses was almost painful. His scent filled her nostrils, clean, animal-hot. His teeth grazed her lobe, his fingers tightened at her nape, and instinctively she turned, seeking his mouth.

His lips were firm, knowing, as they gently pressed hers apart for the slow stroke of his tongue. The taste of him was wild, male, both enticingly strange and unbearably familiar. Her hands found his shoulders, fingers clenching in the soft leather of his jacket. It was cold outside, the air moist and heavy, misting the windows, but she wasn't cold, Blade's heat swamped her, consumed her.

His mouth moved back to her throat, and she shivered at the rough heat of his jaw against her skin, the terrible tension building in her body. She felt cool air against her chest and realised he had pushed up both her sweater and the loose flannel shirt she was wearing beneath. His hands closed on her breasts, and her nipples tightened almost painfully hard against the cotton of her bra.

His gaze locked with hers as he pushed her bra up out of the way; then he bent his head and drew one aching peak into his mouth. She arched, lost to the hot flood of sensation, as the heat twisted and built, clamping tighter and tighter. She felt lush in his hands, feminine and desirable. He moved to her other breast, and she cradled his head, fingers tangled in the warm, thick silk of his hair. He shuddered at the touch, and abruptly she found herself straddling his lap, her breasts naked and damp in the cool night air as he dragged her mouth to his, hands cupping her face as he angled for the kiss, thrusting his tongue deep, penetrating her mouth in a wild, hot rhythm that made her cling to him in an agony of need and despair.

She wanted him.

There was terror and delight in the thought, and a kind of devastating relief. She was alive and female and she wanted Blade to go on touching her, wanted to feel the damp heat blazing off his sleek skin. Her hands bunched in his T-shirt, pulled it free from his jeans so she could slide her palms up beneath the soft cotton. With an impatient growl, Blade jerked the T-shirt off, then her sweater, so that her breasts were pressed against his naked chest.

He kissed her countless times, until she was dazed and aching, her body restless, almost painfully sensitive. Finally he lifted his mouth from hers and pressed her face into his shoulder, holding her against him. Her shirt was wadded uncomfortably. She didn't care; she was incapable of moving. Eventually Anna lifted her head from his shoulder.

Blade was watching her, his eyes shielded by those ridiculously long lashes. "I can't feel the tingle when I touch you now," he said slowly, his fingers stroking the line of her cheek. "I wonder what causes it?"

Anna closed her eyes on a cold ripple of unease. She didn't know what it was herself, beyond some kind of chemistry that existed peculiarly between her and Blade. She wondered what he would say if he found out that maybe the tingle was the result of the strangeness in her, that sometimes her senses were distinctly abnormal, and that she saw and felt in ways that just didn't fit any dictionary definitions of those words?

Chapter 8

Blade parked outside Anna's boarding house and insisted on coming inside with her.

Anna argued, but he wouldn't budge from seeing her to her door. She knew what he would say when he saw the room. The house was a monstrosity. She didn't know how it had escaped being condemned; every part of it that she'd seen was awful. "Down at heel" just didn't cover it.

With a sigh, she unlocked her door, walked inside and flicked on the light. His facial expression didn't change, but inwardly, she cringed. He had to live in lavish wealth, and while that didn't worry her, she was conscious of the ugliness of her surroundings.

"You haven't got a bed," he said slowly. "Where did you sleep last night?"

Anna set her briefcase down, and hung her coat on a hook on the back of the door. Blade could see her sleeping bag; he knew exactly where she'd slept. "The snowfoam cuts the chill.'' She shrugged. ''I was comfortable enough.''

That wasn't a lie. When she'd slept, she had been so exhausted she could have been lying on bare boards and she wouldn't have noticed.

When he spoke, his voice was soft, almost casual. ''How long do you intend to sleep on the floor?''

''Until I can afford to buy a bed.''

''Is Anna your real name?''

Her head snapped up. ''Yes.''

''But Johnson isn't.''

His words broadsided her. He'd done one of those lightning changes, from man to cop—or soldier—the abruptness of it shocking. The calculation of his questioning disturbed her, even though she understood the reason behind it. He knew she was on the run, and he had bided his time all evening, calming her down after her panic in the library, making sure she ate, but now he wanted answers. ''No, Johnson isn't my name.''

When she didn't expand on her answer, he walked over to the window, braced his hand on the lintel and stared out. She knew the questions wouldn't stop, that he would demand to know who she was, why she was on the run, and that she would have to tell him.

Abruptly, he shifted to one side. ''You're coming with me,'' he said flatly, all his attention directed at the street. ''And we're leaving. Now.''

The arrogance of his statement bypassed Anna completely. She was caught and held by the way he'd pulled back from the window, so he could see out, but not be seen. ''What is it? What can you see?''

''Does the name Eric Seber ring a bell?''

Anna shook her head, then realised he wasn't paying

any attention to her; he was still watching the street. "No."

"He searched your flat last night, and right now he's camped out on the road, watching this window."

"How do you know he searched—"

"Because he beat me to it." His gaze connected with hers. "I went back to try and find some trace of where you'd gone, and found Eric already in residence."

His hand curled around her arm, tugging her with him to the door. "We'll go out the back way."

"What about the Jeep?"

"I can get it without Seber realising. He wasn't here when we pulled up, so he won't connect it with you."

As he spoke, he jerked the leather thong from his hair. With the dark mane loose around his shoulders, he looked completely different. Camouflage, she realised, as she snagged her briefcase in passing. The man watching the flat had probably seen Blade, but he had seen either a short-haired man or the ponytail.

They left her light on, then took the stairs and strode the length of a narrow, dark hallway to the rear of the house. The backyard was overgrown, a mass of thick shrubs and weedy lawn. The fence they had to negotiate was a pitiful thing, nothing but rusted strands of wire threading the damp, musty jungle that marked the boundary of both old villas.

They picked their way between skeletal fruit trees, ducked under an oak and walked down a paved lane, ending up on another quiet residential street.

This street was irregularly laid out, so the walk to where the Jeep was parked was convoluted, and longer than they had anticipated.

Blade stopped her beside a tall hedge. "Wait here,
out of sight. I'll collect the Jeep, then pick you up."

He disappeared around the corner. Anna tightened
her grip on her briefcase and pressed back further into
the hedge, wishing she'd thought to grab her coat on
the way out, because it had started to drizzle. The
streetlight at the intersection of the street had dimmed
to little more than a yellowish halo as the drizzle thickened and mist drifted up from the road.

She heard the distant sound of what she thought must
be the Jeep's motor and at the same time heard a faint
movement much closer. She strained to listen, to isolate
the sound. All the hairs at the nape of her neck lifted
in a cold wash of awareness. Suddenly she knew that
the man who had been watching her room was very,
very close. He must have become suspicious, checked
out the rear of the boarding house and spotted them
leaving.

She moved her head slowly, checking first one side
of the street, then the other. It was empty, and for a
moment she was confused. Where was he?

That stark pulse of awareness came again. Very quietly, she stepped out from the hedge, her heart pounding so hard her pulse hammered at the back of her
throat. He was *behind* her, on the other side of the
hedge. She could hear the faint whisper of his tread as
he stepped through wet grass.

Anna glanced around again, quickly running through
her options. She couldn't go in the direction Blade had
gone. The hedge ended in a broad drive a few feet
away. If she crossed that open space the man would
see her, and if he had a gun she would be an easy shot,
silhouetted against the streetlight.

Trying not to make any sound at all, she backtracked, huddling close to the hedge as she searched for a hiding place. All she had to do was keep safe for a few seconds until Blade came. Her sleeve caught on something sharp, distracting her, so that she glanced down. When she checked behind her next, he was there, a blocky figure outlined by dim light.

Cold rain scattered in her face, sending a prickling chill through her. It was the same man who had chased her through Ambrose Park. She saw both arms come up and knew that even though she couldn't see it, he had a gun and was sighting down the barrel before squeezing off a shot.

There was the low growl of an engine, then headlights swept the street, jolting her out of that moment of horrified stasis. Anna lunged sideways, felt the rush of something hot beside her cheek, heard a muffled pop, saw the man waver, turn and take aim at the Jeep.

The headlights snapped off, plunging the street into relative darkness once more. Anna flung herself forward, sprinting onto the road. The Jeep loomed, like a glistening, muscular, black beast. She heard the sound of tires grabbing at the slick surface of the road. A door was flung open, hitting her chest so that she reeled and almost lost her footing. She grabbed at the glint of silver she knew was the handle and threw her briefcase in. There was a muffled curse, a big hand closed around her wrist and she was yanked, sprawling, into the passenger seat. The Jeep shot forward. Anna could feel Blade's hand locked into her sweater, holding her in place as he took a corner at high speed.

She clawed for balance, finally getting her legs beneath her. He released his hold, and she scrambled around so that she was sitting in the seat. Her door banged shut, cutting the roar of the engine. Blade slowed, turned into yet another street, changed gear and flicked a switch. The serene neighbourhood was abruptly illuminated in the sweep of the Jeep's powerful headlights.

He pulled over beneath the glare of a street lamp, jamming on the brakes so that the Jeep rocked to a halt.

"Did he get you?" he demanded, grasping her arms, pulling her around so he could examine her.

Anna recalled the rush of heat beside her cheek, the popping sound. Seber must have shot at her.

"He missed," she said hollowly, wondering why she couldn't feel more.

His grip tightened until it was almost bruisingly hard. Then he leaned down and put his mouth on hers. She opened for him, shuddering beneath the raw force of the kiss, dazedly aware that he needed reassurance. The cold numbness splintered as she realised how close she had come to dying. Blade had saved her, but he had almost been too late.

With a convulsive movement, she threw her arms around his neck, needing to hold him close. Seber had also aimed at Blade. She didn't know if he had gotten off another shot, because the roar of the Jeep had filled her ears, and then Blade had cut the lights and spoiled his aim.

The kiss ended almost as abruptly as it had started. Blade fastened her seatbelt, then pulled back out onto the road. His expression was set, his eyes glittering whenever they met hers.

Anna lifted her fingers to her lips; they felt slightly swollen and tingled with warmth. "Where are we going?"

"My place. And when we get there, you are going

to tell me why a hired gun like Eric Seber keeps drawing a bead on you. Was he the reason you ended up in that ditch in Ambrose Park?''

His voice was deep and very, very calm. Anna decided that she preferred Blade hot and wild and roaring at her to this icy control. ''I didn't know his name,'' she admitted, ''but I recognised him.''

Minutes later, Blade pulled into a reserved space in the car park of the Lombard Hotel. As he swung out of the cab, Anna watched a lean man with distinctive wings of silver at his temples detach himself from an elegant group of people. He was in evening dress and had obviously been attending either a formal dinner or some charity function at the hotel.

The man was backlit so that everything but the silvery hair at his temples was shadowed. As he strode closer, lamplight slid across his high, ascetic cheekbones, the cold, green eyes, his beautifully carved mouth.

Henry de Rocheford.

Anna was frozen in place, numb with shock at the chance meeting. She hadn't seen Henry in years, other than in newspaper clippings, and a distant part of her took in the changes, the thinning of his face, the harsher lines that somehow made him look even more distinguished.

The skin at the base of her neck began to crawl, and rage unfurled deep in her belly. He should look like a monster, she thought dimly. Something of what he was should show. Then her survival instincts kicked in, and she ducked down beneath the dash, huddling into a ball.

Blade turned to lock his door and from his angle

caught the gleam of light sliding over Anna's hair as she crawled under the dash.

"Lombard," de Rocheford said in smooth greeting. "I expected to see you at the fundraiser tonight."

"De Rocheford," Blade acknowledged, barely concealing his impatience. "I had planned to attend. Something came up."

And right now that "something" was doing her level best to mould herself to the underside of the Jeep's dash.

De Rocheford made a few bland enquiries about Blade's family, which he answered, but his mind was working furiously. The newspaper clipping he had picked up in the library popped into his mind. It had been about the Tarrant family and de Rocheford. Blade had assumed the story had been on the back of whatever article she had cut from the paper.

Abruptly, the connection formed in his mind, so obvious, he wondered he hadn't stumbled on it before.

Those distinctive grey eyes, the sense of familiarity that had pulled at him. He had seen Anna before, years ago. It was no wonder he hadn't recognised her. She had been a child then, but even as a kid, she'd been arresting, with that dark copper hair and those solemn eyes, the promise of her mother's exquisite bone structure.

Anna. Anna Tarrant.

She was the missing Tarrant heiress, and if he wasn't mistaken, de Rocheford was the man she was running from. Blade leaned against the Jeep, his expression neutral, and took a damn good look at a man he'd never noticed much before, and never liked.

De Rocheford finally left. Blade waited until the Mercedes glided out of the car park; then he went around and jerked Anna's door open. He stared grimly at her huddled figure. "You can come out now."

"He's gone?"

"He's gone." Blade helped her out, controlling his fury at the magnitude of what she'd hidden from him.

He had been worried that she was a criminal, and she was a damn heiress, probably at least as wealthy as he was. He wanted to shake her for keeping so much from him, and he wanted to push her up against the Jeep and kiss her in sheer relief because at last he knew what she was running from.

He clamped his jaw and did neither, his eyes narrowed as he watched her retrieve her briefcase. A nerve pulsed along his jaw. If she loved him as much as she loved that briefcase, he thought grimly, he would be a happy man. Her movements were surprisingly steady, her expression blankly serene, as if she had spent the evening quietly reading at the library instead of dodging bullets. She was as elegantly graceful and independent as a cat, but she had lost another one of her lives tonight.

Blade gritted his teeth and reminded himself that she was tougher than she looked. He might want to wrap her up in cottonwool, but she wouldn't stay there. She had been on the run for years, fooling everyone into thinking she had died in a car crash so she could be safe. She had eluded a hit man twice—that he knew of—and survived under conditions that would have broken most men, let alone a physically weaker woman from a background of pampered wealth. Blade knew experienced, savvy, deep-cover agents who had cried to have their lives back after two years under another identity. Anna had been in the equivalent of deep cover for something like seven years and she had endured.

Oh, yeah, he wanted to shake her for keeping him in the dark, but more than that, he wanted to kill de Rocheford.

"Don't you want to know why I was hiding from de Rocheford?"

Her voice was as pleasantly modulated as if she were asking him if he wanted a cucumber sandwich with his tea. Blade kept a tight lid on his rage as he locked the vehicle. "You're Anna Tarrant," he rasped.

Anna eyed him warily, noting the muscle jumping along his jaw. "You're mad at me."

"Unless you want a stand-up fight in the car park," he said with dangerous softness, "we'll talk about it inside." He took her arm in a firm grip.

"You don't need to frog-march me," she snapped, jerking free.

Blade slowed, but his annoyance didn't lessen. She could feel the hot simmer of it beneath the cold layers of his control. He wouldn't yell or resort to violence; the angrier he got, it seemed the colder he became. Anna wondered what it would take to rip that control away completely, then decided that no sane person would want to find that out.

He took her through a back entrance, then up a private lift to what turned out to be a penthouse suite.

The room she stepped into was large, but more comfortable than opulent, walls painted a mellow ochre, thick carpet that felt soft enough to sleep on, and several leather couches and easy chairs grouped around a coffee table. A dining table occupied one roomy corner, and bookshelves lined one entire wall. A wooden box crammed with toys occupied one corner, as if children were regular visitors here.

The easy welcome of the room made her throat

tighten with an unexpected pang of emotion. It wasn't the impersonal hotel suite she had expected; it was a home.

It had been a very long time since she had walked into a home.

She noticed a shelf festooned with colourful plants and walked toward them, wondering if she was seeing things. "What are these doing here?"

They were hers. She would have recognised the pots, even if she hadn't recognised the plants.

"When Seber broke into your flat, he made a mess."

"You saved my plants." She stared at Blade, grappling with this added layer to his personality, and touched almost to tears because she *loved* her plants and had hated leaving them behind. It was hard to imagine Blade stopping to do something so…domestic.

But Blade's attention wasn't on her plants. "You're hurt."

His hand closed around her wrist, and he pushed back her sweater sleeve. She had a deep, ragged scratch. Blood had run in thin rivulets, spattering her jersey, soaking the sleeve of her shirt. She vaguely remembered catching her clothing on something thorny as she'd run from Seber—a rose stem, maybe.

"It's nothing," she muttered, pulling her wrist free, prepared to ignore the injury, apart from washing it, because on the scale of things the scratch *was* nothing. "You wanted to talk, so let's get it over with."

Tiredness suddenly overwhelmed her. Her legs felt rubbery, uncoordinated; it was all she could do to cover the short distance to the nearest couch and set her briefcase on the coffee table. She knew it was the adrenalin crash. Two adrenalin crashes, but then, she thought wearily, who was counting?

She perched on the edge of the couch, resisting the urge to relax. If she sank down into that soft leather, she would go to sleep.

Flipping the briefcase open, she began laying out the contents. The items were pitifully few, and shabby: an aging laptop computer she had bought second-hand, the newspaper clippings he'd already spotted in the library—now sadly crumpled—a battered passport, a couple of old credit cards, a heavy gold signet ring.

She held the ring up, watched the light glow on the rich, smooth contours, shimmer off the black onyx inset with initials and a crest worked in gold. "My father's ring."

Her fingers closed around it, making a fist. "Henry stole it." She calmly met Blade's gaze. "I stole it back. I couldn't stand seeing it on his finger. He had no right to it."

"If the ring belonged to your father, then it's yours. You didn't steal it."

"No." Her voice felt raspy, rubbed raw and drained of all emotion. "Henry's taken everything else, but the ring is mine."

She stared at the pitiful items on the table, took a deep breath and made a start. "Henry married my mother, Eloise, about a year after my father died. Then he took my mother and me away from everyone we knew. He isolated us, literally locked us up in his fortress for years. No one came to visit, and as far as I know, no one ever asked about us. It was as if we'd ceased to exist. He never took my mother anywhere, explaining that she 'wasn't well'. He made sure everyone understood that Eloise was mentally unbalanced, and that her daughter was shaping up to be even crazier. The only reason I got out at all was that he couldn't find a legitimate way to keep me out of school and still maintain the fiction that he was caring for us.''

She felt the couch shift as Blade sat down beside her. Calmly, he lifted her onto his lap.

''It's all right,'' he said, when she stiffened in sheer surprise; she had thought he was furious with her. ''Relax,'' he murmured, ''I'm just going to hold you, nothing else.''

He sat back deeper into the couch, the movement making her fetch up against his chest. His arms folded around her, holding her snug against him. After a startled few seconds, Anna began to relax and let her head rest against his shoulder. The steady beat of his heart vibrated through her, oddly comforting when she considered that every one of her encounters with Blade so far had been fraught with tension.

''Henry first tried to kill me when I was eleven,'' she said calmly. ''No-one would believe he'd pushed me into that river. It was so much easier to think that I'd slipped. There were other attempts over the years, but I managed to survive each one.''

''The concussions?''

Anna was startled by the harshness of Blade's voice. ''Yes. Henry needed my death to look like an accident, so he was constrained in his attempts. The first three times I tried to convince the local police that what had happened to me hadn't been an accident. They looked into it each time, but Henry was very plausible. In the end, they thought I was a loon—as loony as Henry had convinced everyone my mother was. I became a standing joke in the community. People would stop and point at me and say, 'There goes that crazy Tarrant kid.'''

She told him about the accident that had convinced

her she should disappear until she was old enough to claim control of Tarrant Holdings, Henry's legal notice petitioning to have her declared dead, and her efforts to contact the Tarrant lawyers, ending with the Ambrose Park incident.

"Have you been to the police about that?"

"Not yet." Anna pushed away enough so that she could meet his gaze. "You believe me?"

She had to see for herself, because for years she hadn't been believed, and it had never been more important to her.

Blade's gaze was direct, unflinching. "I believe you," he said curtly. "But I could damn well shake you for not telling me this sooner. You nearly died tonight. I nearly lost you."

"Would it have mattered?"

"Yes," he said from between clenched teeth, "it would have mattered."

Emotion welled in Anna, sharp and piercing. It wasn't exactly a declaration of love, but then, she hadn't expected one. At least he believed her.

Blade caught hold of her wrist and turned her arm over so he could examine the scratch. Blood was still leaking sullenly where her sweater kept scraping against the jagged rip. "You need that cut seen to."

"I'll clean it in the shower." Anna looked down at her damp, muddy, blood-spattered clothes. "I don't suppose you have something I could wear?"

His attention focused on her with a possessive intensity. "I'll get you one of my shirts."

Abruptly, he set her away from him and disappeared into a bedroom. He reappeared with a soft, faded chambray shirt in one hand, then showed her to a bathroom sleek with creamy marble and huge well-lit mirrors—the first signs of opulence she'd seen.

"When you're decent, let me know and I'll dress that cut."

He met her gaze in the mirror, and she read his intent. It was easy, because he did nothing to hide his satisfaction that she was in his home, that after she had showered, the only clothes she would have worth wearing would be his. He hadn't said where she would sleep, but she had noticed several doors in the suite, so some of them had to be extra bedrooms. If she wanted, she could have a room to herself; Blade wouldn't force her to share his bed. Not that force would even enter the equation. He had ruthlessly pursued her, kicked all her defences aside; he could have made love to her in the front seat of his Jeep if he'd wanted. He might not know that she'd fallen in love with him, but she wouldn't be able to hide it from him for long.

His dark gaze was flat with certainty, and for good reason. He was going to have her naked beneath him tonight, and they both knew it.

Chapter 9

While Anna was in the shower, Blade took note of the two-hour time difference and rang his brother, Gray, at his home in Sydney.

After several rings, Gray finally picked up.

"What took you so long?"

There was a vague shuffling sound, then Gray said, "Hear that?"

Blade heard muffled hiccupy sounds. "My niece," he murmured. Gray and his wife Sam had had twins just six months before.

"Your nephew," Gray corrected. "He's teething."

"Is that allowed at six months?"

"Not in my rule book. We just got them to sleep through the night. Why are you ringing? Don't tell me the hotel's burned down, because if it has, Sam will make me build it again."

Blade grinned. Gray and Sam had had a long, interrupted courtship that had finally come together at the then Pacific Royal hotel, a crumbling Victorian ruin Lombards had bought specifically for the location. Gray's plans to demolish the building had hit a snag when he had realised how attached Sam was to the old building and to the people she worked with there.

Blade cut straight to the point. "Remember the Tarrants?"

"Tarrant Holdings. Yeah, Dad used to do business with Hugh Tarrant. When Hugh died, Henry de Rocheford took control of the company. Eloise died a few months ago. The daughter, Anna, died several years ago."

Blade used the same tactic Gray had used with his nephew, he held the phone out toward the shower. "Hear that? That's the sound of Anna Tarrant using my shower."

There was a small silence, filled by another distant hiccup and a rustling of cloth. "How do you know it's her?"

"It's her." Blade let the certainty of his statement sink in. He briefly ran through how he'd first found Anna and the sequence of events since then. "She's got credit cards, a signet ring with Hugh Tarrant's initials and the Tarrant crest engraved on it, and a passport. She's changed from the passport photo, but then, she is seven years older. The similarity is still striking."

"She could have stolen those things."

"It's her, Gray. Don't ask me how I know, but it *is* Anna Tarrant."

"You're sleeping with her."

Blade swore softly beneath his breath. "Not yet," he muttered. He filled Gray in on the night's events and the motivation behind them, fingers tightening on the receiver. When he'd driven around the corner and seen Seber lift his gun and take aim at Anna, he had been poleaxed by fear.

"What do you need me to do?" Gray asked flatly.

Blade leaned back in his chair. That was Gray, straight for the throat. "I need you to use your resources and pull all the information you can on de Rocheford and Seber, and anything to do with the Tarrant family or Tarrant Holdings. I'd like to know exactly what I'm going up against here."

"Have you involved the police yet?"

"We'll do that tomorrow. It's almost midnight here, and Anna needs sleep more than she needs to spend the next few hours kicking her heels in a police interview room. Besides, I don't like exposing her until I know more. So far we don't have one piece of solid evidence that he's trying to kill her, only Anna's testimony, and to get that to stick, we've got to prove her identity first. If I can connect Seber to de Rocheford, he's history."

Gray asked for more specific details and made notes. "Henry was Hugh Tarrant's stepbrother," he said thoughtfully, "but he's no actual blood relation to the Tarrants. From memory, Henry's father was killed in one of the Tarrant mines, and old man Tarrant married Henry's mother but never adopted Henry. When Hugh was born he became sole heir to Tarrant Holdings. When Hugh was killed—also in a mining accident— Henry married *his* widow." Gray paused. "There's a certain…symmetry to the situation."

"As in Henry saw his chance to grab everything he'd only ever been allowed to look at."

"And if he blamed Tarrants for his father's death in

the first place, then that might be even more motive for hurting the Tarrant women.''

Blade's stomach tightened when he thought of exactly how de Rocheford had abused the Tarrant women. He had to wonder if Eloise Tarrant's death had been the accidental overdose that was reported. ''That man is sicker than I thought,'' he said grimly.

''I'll e-mail you whatever I can find tomorrow. And Blade...I don't know de Rocheford that well, I doubt anyone does, but he's a cold, efficient bastard when it comes to business. Watch your back.''

''Don't worry about my back—it's going to be plenty covered.''

Blade heard someone else speak to Gray.

Gray then came back on the line, his rough voice laced with amusement. ''Sam wants to know when we're likely to meet this woman. She says Mom's fretting about your long hair and the earring, and Aunt Sophie swears she saw you in some X-rated movie. Sophie's telling all her friends that that stud farm you bought doesn't have a thing to do with horses.''

Blade groaned. ''What about my lethal weapon status?''

''You've still got that, mate. They're just talking different equipment.''

Anna rinsed her hair clean of conditioner, and then stood beneath the wonderfully hot stream of water and washed out her bra and panties.

She toweled herself dry, wound the towel around herself, then searched for a hair dryer, which she found in a cupboard, along with a magazine that had been folded open.

Anna read the article as she dried her hair. There

was a photo of Blade in evening dress. Clinging to his arm was a beautiful blonde in almost no dress at all. Anna's eyes narrowed at the satisfied look on Blade's face; he looked like a big, happy panther who'd just found a new kitty to play with. She scowled and tossed the magazine back in the cupboard, temper smouldering. Her confidence with men was zero. The last thing she'd needed was a glance at the competition, and according to the story, there had been a great deal of competition.

The story might have been made up, but she wasn't willing to bet on it. Women would swarm all over Blade, wanting to run their fingers through his silky hair and touch his big muscles. Wanting to know what that beautiful mouth felt like on theirs.

The fierceness of her jealousy took her by surprise, but she didn't pull back from it. She examined her response and decided that whether she had confidence and experience with men or not wasn't an issue. The hell with it. She was in love with Blade, and she wasn't prepared to share.

When she slipped into the shirt, she found that it was more than just big, it swamped her. The tails fell to her knees and the sleeves hung well below her wrists, so that she had to roll them back almost to the shoulder seams. It also smelled subtly of Blade, despite the fresh overlay of laundry detergent.

A delicate tension gripped her, as the suffocating intimacy of the situation hit. Her heart began to pound in sheer panic. Even though she had decided to make love with Blade, the risk she was taking was frightening. All her life she had been losing people she loved; her father, her grandmother, finally her mother. She had lost her puppy to the same river that had nearly claimed her and pledged never to have another pet—never love a pet—that Henry could destroy. She had existed in a void of her own making, carefully guarding herself against the anguish of loss.

It had been a cowardly, empty existence, but it had been safe.

Tonight, Seber had shown her just how empty her safe life had been. When he had lifted that gun in Blade's direction, she'd discovered that nothing mattered to her as much as Blade. Not her identity, not all her lost years or her emotional safety. The threat of Blade's death had shoved everything into a sharp, new perspective.

She no longer cared if she had only a limited time with Blade. She was through with hiding, through with protecting herself. If a small piece of his life was all she could have, then she was taking it.

Anna stared at herself in the mirror. Her hair hung loose and straight, her eyes were dark with excitement. She wondered how she could bear to let him see her like this. She wasn't naked. Shrouded in his shirt, without panties, she felt worse than naked.

When she walked into the lounge, Blade was seated at a desk in a corner alcove, all his concentration taken by a computer screen. She noticed he had changed his clothes, although he was still wearing jeans and a T-shirt. He also looked freshly showered, his hair still sleek with moisture. She realised there must be another bathroom in the suite, and some of her tension drained away. Blade had chosen to shower separately, letting her have her privacy. The consideration of that small act was subtly reassuring. He might be blunt in his intentions, but he wouldn't crudely rush her into bed.

When he saw her, he immediately hit the screen saver and strolled over to the couches. There was a first-aid box already set out on the coffee table.

Anna perched on the edge of a couch. Blade sat down on the coffee table and placed her forearm across his thigh.

He tipped disinfectant onto a pad of cottonwool, but before he applied it to the scratch, he caught her gaze and held it. "You recognised me that first night. Why didn't you tell me who you were? I knew you when you were a kid. Our families knew each other. I patched up your knee once. You could have trusted me."

"You remember the knee?"

"Looks like we both do. So why didn't you tell me?"

She gritted her teeth against the sting as he cleaned the scratch. "I couldn't figure out a reasonable explanation for why you had found me in Ambrose Park. I still don't know how you did it."

If she thought he was going to tell her, he thought wryly, she was wrong. He reached for a tube of ointment and smoothed it on the scratch.

A yawn took her by surprise. "I was suspicious of everybody. I couldn't afford not to be."

His gaze pinned her. "Do you trust me now?"

"Yes."

Blade controlled the extent of his relief, his exaltation that he had finally gained her trust—even if he still had the feeling he'd forced her into it. He finished the dressing and rose to his feet. She was still wary, and bone tired.

He wanted to take her to bed tonight. He had planned to take her to bed. He was burning up inside, his arousal hard and painful, his skin hot and sensitive, but he knew now he wasn't going to do it.

Anna was exhausted, her eyes drooping with fatigue. The rich coppery gleam in her hair made her skin look almost translucently pale. The yellowish bruise on her forehead and the bandage on her arm made her look even more fragile. She needed to sleep, and if she got into bed with him, they wouldn't be doing much sleeping.

He had wanted Anna and ruthlessly set out to have her. She was with him now, but he'd found out almost nothing about her likes and dislikes, what she liked to read, what music she listened to. He had almost lost her twice in the space of two days.

Two days! The short span of time stunned Blade, even as he acknowledged its relative unimportance. He had known more beautiful women than Anna over a period of years, women who had made it clear they were available to him, yet who had left him cold emotionally. Anna had stirred him from the first. Even without the added mystery and frustration of the dreams, he would have wanted her.

Having her sleeping so close to him, yet not in his bed, was going to be torture. He knew that once he had Anna in his bed, she wouldn't find it easy to leave him. For Anna, making love would be a commitment, and he was determined to use it to bind her to him. But not at the expense of her trust.

He felt a moment of incredulity that he was actually reduced to this kind of manipulation to keep a woman. There was a word for it, and that word was "desperate."

She was watching him sleepily, still perched on the

edge of the couch, as if afraid that the second she relaxed he would be on her. She wasn't far wrong.

"I'll go and make your bed up. You look dead on
your feet."

Her eyes widened in surprise, but her reaction was
dazed, so far gone with fatigue she could barely function. When he came back from putting fresh sheets on
the bed in the room he'd chosen for her, she was curled
up asleep, her cheek resting on one arm of the couch,
her knees drawn up beneath his shirt, so that only the
toes of one foot peeked out.

Blade shook her gently, and when she didn't rouse,
bent and lifted her into his arms. She was as light as a
child, baby-soft and gently curved. It seemed incredible
to Blade that she had eluded Henry for so many years,
escaped death so many times.

Her head lolled against his shoulder, hair spilling in
a fragrant tumble, lashes dark against her skin. She
muttered something indistinct, and he automatically
cradled her closer, soothing her with his voice. She
nuzzled into his chest, cuddling closer still, as if she
needed to be touched, needed to be held; then she relaxed back into boneless sleep.

Blade's gaze fixed on her mouth, and his stomach
clenched in a mixture of tenderness and gut-wrenching
desire. He'd kissed her tonight and lost control like a
teenager; he had been close to making love to her in
the cab of the Jeep, where any passer-by could have
seen what was happening. Although the windows had
been steamed up. It had been an all-round steamy situation.

Anna hadn't attempted to stop him, although she was
still wary of him.

The wariness cut both ways. He carried her to her

bed and gently tucked her in. What she had told him about her past tallied with the dreams he'd had, which meant everything he had ''dreamed'' or ''seen'' at various times had been real.

He didn't know how it happened, or why he was the recipient of whatever Anna ''broadcasted,'' but he didn't like it.

As fiercely as he was drawn to Anna, as much as he cared for her, he didn't want anyone messing with his mind.

Eric Seber pulled his car into the breakdown lane and parked. He sat, considering the torrential rain exploding off his windscreen, the careening headlights as traffic spilled down the motorway like brilliantly lighted flotsam skimming the surface of a river in full flood. Stoically, he considered his second mistake.

He had been made.

The big dark guy with Anna Johnson had been savvy. He'd been taken by surprise. Apart from the one incident just days ago, when Anna Johnson had eluded him, that hadn't happened for years. Seber didn't like surprises; he liked being alive better.

The windscreen began to fog. Methodically, he flicked the fan on full and adjusted it to demist; then he picked up his mobile phone. He had made a second mistake, this one with stronger repercussions. He couldn't assume that Anna Johnson and the guy she was with couldn't describe him.

De Rocheford picked up on the fourth ring.

Seber listened as his client rolled out his name. The man had a voice like a radio personality or a television presenter. He enunciated ''de Rocheford'' as if he were presenting it as a damn gift, all trussed up with a satin bow and coated in cream. Seber normally didn't waste much time thinking about any of his clients after he'd checked them out to his satisfaction, but de Rocheford had got under his skin from the first. Money aside, the slick bastard was a pain in the ass.

He made his report.

There was a lengthy silence. The demister whirred loudly; the condensation on the window was clearing in patches.

"You say she had a man with her?"

Seber noticed that this time there was no cream coating de Rocheford's voice. "Yeah. Big stud, with long black hair, looked familiar, but I can't quite place him. Drove a black Jeep, late model. I got a partial on the plates."

De Rocheford bit out a short, hard word.

Seber would have smiled if he hadn't been so ticked himself. Now the great man was using the "f" word.

"I think I know who she's with," said de Rocheford. "Give me what you've got on the plates and I'll check it out. Meet me at my house. Now."

Seber stiffened. He only met clients once, for an initial consultation at a location of his choosing. He liked to keep his anonymity firmly in place, structure the payments so he didn't get ripped off, and do the job clean and neat. He also liked to tape his clients as a little additional insurance, just in case they tried to change the rules. Coldly, he eyed the glistening stream of traffic that had slowed to a crawl. "That's not in our agreement."

De Rocheford told him what he could do with the agreement.

Seber took it on the jaw. Reluctantly, he repeated the two letters and one number he'd managed to get on the Jeep, then took down de Rocheford's address. He had made the mistakes; it was up to him to fix the situation. If that meant meeting with de Rocheford again, he had no choice. If word got around that he didn't meet his obligations, he was washed up in this line of work. But he didn't have to like it. Meeting de Rocheford would expose him needlessly, and he'd already caught a police tail on him more than once. Damn.

De Rocheford had said he thought he knew who Anna Johnson was with, and now Seber was willing to bet he wanted another kill. Seber had a bad feeling about this; nothing had gone according to plan. All he wanted to do was put distance between himself and de Rocheford, ditch this car and disappear for a while.

Resolutely, he consulted his road map and pulled out onto the highway, aimed in a direction he didn't want to go. He would meet with de Rocheford and rectify his mistakes. His mind automatically ran through a list of useful contacts he periodically used when he needed backup.

When the job was done, he would collect his payment, liquidate his assets and leave the country.

And before he went, he decided, he might do de Rocheford, too. Just for the hell of it.

Chapter 10

The dream seeped into Blade's consciousness sometime in the dark hours before dawn.

It was Anna, his ghost, the woman who had haunted him for more years than he cared to count. The woman who had frustrated him. Tormented him. Made him furious. Made him long for her.

He felt her touch, whisper-soft. She brushed close, then pressed against him, her skin silky smooth, soft and cool. His hands settled at her waist, anticipation tightening every muscle in his body as his nostrils flared, drinking in the female scent of her.

She was bolder than she'd ever been before, winding her arms around his neck and reaching up to kiss his mouth, his jaw, his neck. Her expression was dreamy, absorbed as her hands slid smoothly over his skin, examining him, petting him.

His breath rasped inwards when she reached down

and cupped him, wrapping around the broad base of his shaft, stroking gently, until he was heavy and throbbing, and he had to wonder if this time he would go mad, if this time he would lose control.

Desire poured through him, filled him, until he had to set his teeth against the aching need to pull her close and make love to her without preliminaries—without even the barest foreplay. His hands had tightened on her waist, and he was lifting her, before he brought himself under control.

Her hands gripped his shoulders. The silken swath of her hair swung against his jaw, and her breasts brushed his chest, the nipples firm. Heat rolled through him, wrenching a groan from deep in his belly.

He clasped her buttocks, encouraging her to wrap her legs around his waist. Her arms twined his neck as she buried her face against his shoulder.

He cupped her nape, dragging her mouth to his. She came without resistance, hungry for his touch. A shudder rippled through him as her mouth parted beneath his. He reached down without preliminaries and guided himself to her opening, felt her readiness for *him*.

Blade had been wanted by many women, but to his knowledge, he had never been *needed* like this. Her need was seductive, fierce; it undermined him as nothing else could, and it matched his own.

It was his own need that confused him the most, because it bound him to her, chained him as effectively as if he'd been manacled to her side. He couldn't feel this way for anyone else, couldn't desire any other woman the way he desired Anna.

Her mouth glided over his, clung, soft, lush, hesitant, and his attention shifted.

"Do it," he demanded.

Her mouth nuzzled his lips apart. He felt the tentative incursion of her tongue, shyly stroking against his. Her taste shimmered through him, and his knees almost buckled, the pleasure of that simple caress dizzying. *"Yes."*

Her very directness and lack of guile cut through Blade's defences, breached his control. If she had been skilful in the art of seduction, a part of him would always have held back. He was too well-versed in the subtle nuances of relationship games to be controlled by sex.

Her fingers clenched in his hair as he began to enter her. The constriction made him break out in a sweat, his heart pounding, dark heat flushing his skin as he withdrew, then shoved deep. She arched on a shivering cry and he bent and closed his mouth over one beaded nipple, suckling gently. He felt the moment when she tightened almost painfully hard around him, the wild, convulsive clenching of delicate inner muscles. He shuddered, cradling her close, straining against his own incipient release, straining not to lose himself in the shuddering whirlpool of need.

Anna came awake, a cry echoing in the stillness of her room. Her cheeks were cold, and she was startled to find them wet with tears. She jackknifed upright, hugging her knees, burying her face in the covers. The rest of her wasn't cold. She was hot, aching inside, the emptiness between her legs throbbing.

Blade.

Her head came up. She stared wildly, searching every corner of the room. It was empty, but his presence was a palpable weight. The dream had been powerful, *real*....

She climbed out of the tangled nest she'd made of the bed and stumbled to the bifold doors, shoving back the filmy sheers so that moonlight flooded the room more brightly. It had stopped raining, although the terrace still gleamed with moisture. She opened the doors and stepped outside.

It was cold and clear, the sky a glittering bed of stars in stark contrast to the murky, violent squall that had swept through just hours before. She welcomed the chill, the icy cut of the breeze.

She lifted a hand to push hair back from her face and considered the dream.

Anna had already faced the fact that the depth of what she felt for Blade might never be returned. Her dream man was a man who had fulfilled many women's fantasies, not just her own. He wanted her. He had been blunt about exactly how much, but that didn't mean he needed her, or that he would want her forever.

But when he left, would she be able to stop dreaming about him? Would she ever be able to get him out of her head?

She stared at the moon and felt hot tears pool in her eyes. Why had she bothered with the question, when she'd known the answer all along? No. She would never forget him, never stop loving him. She had taken one look at him as a child and settled on him then.

She heard a sound and turned. Blade was walking toward her, clad in nothing but a pair of jeans. Her gaze fastened on the broad span of his chest. The sight of his naked torso was subtly shocking.

He stopped just short of touching her, his gaze locked on hers, sharply male, fiercely intent.

"Bad dream?" he enquired on a low, silky rumble, reaching out to cradle her face between both hands.

The deliberation of the act, the warmth of his palms, sent heat flashing through her, along with the knowledge that *he knew.*

He knew about the dreams.

His fingers drifted down her throat, trailing fire, then paused between her breasts, so that they swelled and throbbed. Anna went rigid with shock as he began undoing her shirt buttons.

Her hands clamped over his. "What are you doing?" Her voice was thin, strained.

"You called me." His words were soft, biting. "You called me the night I found you in Ambrose Park. You've been calling me for years. Now I'm here."

She shook her head, as much in rejection of what he'd said as of that puzzling, underlying note of fury. "I dreamed—"

His fingers covered her mouth. "We're not going to talk about it." His lashes lowered, shading the hot glitter in his eyes almost completely, but she could feel his ferocious attention centred on her mouth. "We're going to do it."

The low words went through her with the hot, abrupt force of an electric shock. She had wondered what it would take for Blade's control to break, and now she knew.

He was watching her closely, and she realised that despite his raw demand, he was holding back enough to gauge her reaction, giving her a chance to say no.

When she didn't answer, his fingers slipped from her lips and brushed the tangled fall of her hair aside. His palm cupped the tender skin of her nape, urging her closer. She braced her hands against his rib cage. Now that it was finally going to happen, she felt lost and panicky.

He was going to make love to her. He was going to fulfil the fantasy that had haunted her all of her adult life, the fantasy *he* said he had shared in, and she didn't know if she could bear it. The emotions in the dreams were so intense, desperate and wild—the pleasure piercing.

His raw need beat at her, poured over and around her. His focus was wholly on her.

She lifted her face to him. Her gaze was direct, her voice steady. "I'm a virgin."

Shock briefly registered in his gaze. She heard his rough intake of air, then he dropped his forehead until it rested on hers, the gesture oddly whimsical and tender.

"I must be losing my touch. I take it all back, you don't have to do this."

Anna shook her head and deliberately rubbed her hands over his chest, pausing at the tight, hard nubs of his nipples. She felt the tremor that ran through him, and his unexpected vulnerability gave her the courage she needed. "I want to make love with you. I'm going to have what I want for once."

"If you're going to have me at all," he said, lifting her into his arms and carrying her into his room, "I can tell you it's going to be more than once."

He set her down next to the bed, shut the doors

against the cool night air, then jerked all the curtains open, so that moonlight flooded the room.

She watched as he unfastened his jeans, pushed them down his thighs and stepped out of them.

He was beautifully made: his shoulders sleek, his chest broad and beautifully muscled, his stomach flat, hips whipcord lean, flaring to long, powerful legs. In the moonlight, his skin was copper-dark, every lean curve and hard-packed swell of muscle etched in shadowy relief. But it was the centre of his body that compelled her attention and held it. His sex was thick, muscular in appearance, and it jutted boldly from the apex of his thighs.

He came to a halt in front of her, as confident naked as he was dressed, and Anna decided that he had every right to be.

He picked her hand up and wrapped it around the broad base of his arousal in a movement that closely mirrored the dream. A ripple of shock went through her at the unexpected contact, the way his hot flesh bucked beneath her grip.

His hand covered hers before she could pull back. "You didn't hurt me," he murmured. "I liked it."

The texture of him was alien yet fascinating, satin-sleek and pulsing with life, and so incredibly hard. Blade was beautiful in a powerful, masculine way, like a big cat or a blooded stallion, and Anna found she wanted to touch, to stroke, to learn every part of him, but this…this part of him fascinated her.

She was almost twenty-seven; she knew what a naked man looked like, even if she had never had sex, but she had never considered she would find a man's private parts…beautiful. She moved her fingers, stroking the length of him, exploring the solid bluntness of his shape, the silky heat and slickness of his skin. She felt him tighten in her hold, heard his harsh intake of air.

"Next time…" he said hoarsely, stilling her fingers with one hand, then starting on the buttons of her shirt. "Next time you can do anything you want to me."

She felt the shirt slip from her shoulders; then his arms went around her. The shock of him naked against her took her breath. It was like being on fire; every part of her burned.

Something cool brushed the backs of her legs—the coverlet, then Blade was pulling her onto the rumpled bed with him. He bent and kissed her, his weight gradually settled on her, pressing her into the mattress, as his mouth played with hers—long, tender kisses that made her ache with their sweetness, gentle bites and teasing nips, kisses that became increasingly deep and wild, so that she moved restlessly beneath him, testing the resistance of his heavy weight, burying her fingers in his hair.

He nuzzled her neck, trailing downward, the glide of his body against hers an exquisite torment. His mouth fastened on one breast, and she gasped, arching beneath him at the rush of pleasure. He transferred his attention to the other breast, seemingly fascinated by her changing textures, her sensitivity to his touch. She felt the nudge of his knee parting her legs, his hand, heavy on her stomach; then it dipped lower, cupping her.

A shudder went through him. "You're already wet," he said softly.

He continued to kiss her as his fingers parted her folds, and she went still in an agony of apprehension and desperate curiosity, then burning pleasure, as he began gently stroking her. His finger slid into her, probing. He withdrew, then slid into her again, this time with more difficulty. She realised there were two fingers now, moving in a disturbing rhythm, probing deeper each time, gently stretching. He withdrew, and she felt the slick heat of his fingers as he continued to stroke, her whole body arching at the almost unbearable flood of sensation.

Just when she thought she couldn't take any more, he reached down and fitted himself to her opening.

Heat poured through her like the first onslaught of a fever as he pressed inward. He leaned forward, his expression taut, absorbed, as he continued to press into her, rocking gently. Her fingers dug into his shoulders, and she drew her knees up. The movement eased the tight constriction, so that he penetrated her shallowly.

He shuddered in her arms and stilled, his hands cradling her face, gaze fixed on hers, gauging her every reaction. He was holding her as if she would break, holding himself in check, and it ran through her mind that this was completely different to the dreams. The sensations Blade's touch triggered were almost too intense. There was no misty veil, no dream to buffer her now. Everything was sharply edged and vividly real. And the scent… She hadn't known how erotic the hot male scent of him would be. She wanted to be closer, to touch and taste him, breathe him in.

The slow penetration started again, and she tensed, although there was no pain.

The whispery rumble of his voice poured over her,

soothing, enticing. His hands stroked her face, his gaze almost unbearably tender. His weight shifted, easing up on the pressure between her legs. His chest brushed her breasts starting a shimmer of pure delight. One hand gripped her nape, tilting her head back. His mouth came down on hers. He was taut in her arms, fine tremors running beneath his skin, heart slamming heavily in his chest.

She stroked his back and he groaned, almost purring with pleasure. His mouth closed on her breast. The tug of sensation arrowed straight to her loins, shoving her over some invisible line, transforming the faint discomfort of stretching into hot, burning pleasure.

He continued to croon and stroke, encouraged her to stroke him, coaxing, gentling as he rocked, easing himself deeper inside her.

Without warning, the slow building of pressure exploded into searing pleasure and she arched, pressing against him. He went rigid against her. She heard a soft curse, then his hips recoiled and he plunged inside her, gliding deep.

Her fingers sank into Blade's shoulders.

He withdrew and pushed deep again. The hot tingling pleasure intensified, spreading upward, stealing her breath until her lungs ached and her heart pounded, and the night seemed to draw in, no longer cold, but swirling close, a suffocating mantle of darkness.

A rough sound tore from Blade's throat. ''This is...*killing* me.''

The effort of control was etched on his face. His jaw was rigid, the line of his mouth set, as if the control he was enforcing was painful, and suddenly she realised holding back *was* painful for him.

The cords of his neck and shoulders were taut. Sweat sheened his skin, making every movement a fluid shift of copper. A muscle jumped in his jaw as he withdrew, then pushed back in.

The penetration, the raw physicality of the act, was still alien, but the heat and weight of Blade, the piercing tenderness of his gaze holding hers, the intense pleasure of being so close to him, held its own lure. She'd read enough, heard enough, to know that making love was a dicey business and didn't always bring pleasure. She'd dreamed enough to *know* the pleasure. Yet this…she hadn't dreamed this. It was more. There was no other explanation, just more, and it threatened to overwhelm her.

They lay locked together on the rumpled sheets, the room flooded with moonlight.

"Wrap your legs around my waist," he demanded.

Abruptly, he shifted, too, pulling her more firmly beneath him. Anna twined her arms around his neck and held on as his rhythm became shorter, sharper, and once more pleasure coiled through her, catching her by surprise, spinning her off balance.

For a panicked moment, she thought she was falling; then Blade's arms closed around her, anchoring her against him, holding her as the world shimmered out of focus and there was nothing left but the sun exploding inside her, burning away the cold, banishing every last shadow.

Chapter 11

Blade pulled on his jeans and prowled onto the terrace. The moon had set, and rosy dawn lightened the eastern horizon so that the sea shimmered like beaten copper, and the angular shapes of city buildings were softened, as if they were carved from ancient stone instead of more modern materials.

As the sky rapidly lightened, he grimly catalogued the disaster the last few hours had been, from the moment he had chased Anna down in the library to this morning's debacle.

He would have kicked himself if it would have done any good, but he suspected it wouldn't. When it came to Anna, he thought with what was in his pants, not his head.

Tonight she had needed rest, kindness. Protection. She had needed his help. She had been a virgin.

All he had wanted to do was strip her naked and

take her down onto the icy tiles of the terrace. He hadn't been that crude, but it had been a near thing.

He hadn't worn a condom.

He *never* had unprotected sex. The condom had occurred to him, but he had instantly rejected the thought of wearing one. His mind, his whole body, had been on fire, brought to a fever pitch of madness by the dream. He had needed to know that she was feeling *him* inside her. He wouldn't have been able to tolerate even a thin latex barrier between them.

It had flashed through his mind that he wanted to impregnate her, and even that hadn't been enough to stop him. When he had poured himself into Anna's body, the moment had held a primitive power that still shook through him.

The breeze freshened with the dawn, bringing with it the distant, mournful cry of gulls.

The morning hadn't changed a damn thing, he decided bleakly. Even though he knew he should have protected Anna against pregnancy, he still felt a fierce satisfaction that he had probably already impregnated her. If there had ever been a politically correct cell in his body, the wild heat of their lovemaking had incinerated it.

He wanted Anna pregnant. He wanted her bound to him.

If she was pregnant, she would have to marry him.

Satisfaction filled him at the thought. The decision felt right. It wasn't as if they were strangers; they had known each other for years. They'd been making love to each other for years. The ring on her finger was just a damn detail.

He felt her presence behind him and half turned, one

hand wrapped around the railing. He studied her rumpled hair, pale skin, the shadows beneath her eyes. "Are you all right?"

"Yes."

The answer was unequivocal, and it startled him.

She walked toward him, once more dressed in his shirt. Her step was a little uneven, as if she was tender from his lovemaking. Not a big surprise, when he had all but attacked her.

She hesitated, then took a last step and slid her arms around his waist, cuddling in against his chest. "I love you."

Blade stiffened with surprise. His hands settled on her shoulders. He wanted to crush her to him, he wanted to take her back to bed. "I shouldn't have touched you."

She tipped her head back, her expression changing from soft to guarded. "Why not?"

"Because my control was...questionable. Because you were exhausted and needed to sleep."

"I'm not made of porcelain. I didn't break."

His brows jerked together. Didn't she have any sense? "I could have hurt you."

She frowned and stepped back from him, dislodging his hold. "You didn't hurt me. I *liked* what you did. But that's not what we need to talk about." She hugged the shirt to her chest, and her expression smoothed out to the remoteness he disliked so much. "You said you found me in Ambrose Park because I called out to you. I need to know what you meant by that."

Blade propped himself against the railing and folded his arms across his chest. "I had a dream about a woman running through mist and rain. She was being hunted. I knew she was hurt, that she had fallen. She called out to me for help, and for the first time I had a clue I could use. One of the images that flashed into my mind was the Gamezone sign. I looked it up in the telephone book and came searching until I found you.''

His gaze narrowed on her face. Her features were so calm and still, she could have been moulded from porcelain. "I've thought this through, and the only answer has to be that you have some kind of psychic talent that somehow relates to a mental link with me. It's my guess that you broadcast and I pick it up. However it works, I've been having visions, sharing in your dreams, since I was about sixteen. The first bad one was when you were just a kid and were swept away in a river, on the point of drowning. I've had several like that. A burning house, a fall down a cliff. You were hit by a car once." He paused. "There was another accident with a car, but I don't know what happened—the images stopped."

His head came up sharply. "The car going over the cliff. The accident that was supposed to have killed you."

Anna rubbed her hands up her arms, as if the memory chilled her. "Henry came back later and finished the job by pushing the car over the cliff and saying I must have been in it."

"That would explain why I didn't dream any more. The danger was over. You stopped broadcasting."

She stared at him steadily. "I didn't know I could do any of that. When I thought of you, called out to you or dreamed of you, I didn't know anything was happening! I thought you were just a fantasy inside my head. There have been people in my family with psychic talent, but I didn't think I'd inherited anything much.''

"What else can you do?" It came out sharply, but Blade was too edgy to soften the demand. When it came down to it, he was a plain old-fashioned kind of guy; he liked logic and clean explanations. If there was anything weird happening, his first instinct was to strip it down to its essential components—like a car engine—and examine how it worked. But he couldn't do that here, because he didn't know the first thing about any of this.

"I'm not a trick dog," she snapped. "I...feel things.''

He waited, every muscle in his body tensed.

Her expression closed up again, her eyes going blank so he couldn't read what she was thinking. It perversely irritated him, even though he knew he was the cause of it.

"Don't worry," she said, as cool as ice. "I won't grow another head.''

Suddenly Blade could hear in her voice the expensive finishing school she must have attended, see the haughty disdain in the tilt of her chin. He felt briefly knocked off balance. He didn't know how he could ever have missed what she was: a lady—from the top of her silky head to the tips of her dainty toes.

"I can pick up on moods sometimes," she said abruptly, staring somewhere just left of his shoulder, "but usually only if the emotion is strong, and directed at me. I never thought of it as anything too unusual, an amplification of what everyone picks up from body language and speech, but I guess it *is* strange. I knew Henry hated me when I was quite small.'' Her eyes challenged him. "He hated that I knew what he was feeling, that he couldn't hide it from me."

"I don't like it, either," Blade admitted. "Can you control it?"

Her eyes narrowed on him, steel grey, not a sign of mist to be seen. "I don't know," she said flatly.

Even though she had braced herself for it, his rejection of how different she was still hurt. He wanted her, even needed her to some extent, but he had yet to accept—and maybe would never fully accept—what she was. *She* was still reeling from discovering the dreams had been real, and she had been brought up in a family that expected psychic talents.

"It doesn't matter." His hands closed on her shoulders. "We'll work it out."

His touch burst through her on an aching rush of sweet warmth. It was all she could do not to throw herself into his arms and say, "Yes, we can work it out. I know I'm weird, but, hey, I can change just for you." The reality was that she couldn't change; she couldn't turn off what happened in her head. "I'm used to taking care of myself."

"You're used to running. There's a difference."

She stiffened. "Says who?"

"How many times have you almost died?"

"I try not to keep count. It could get depressing."

His teeth came together with an audible snap. "*I've* been counting. Lady, there is no way I'm letting you out of my sight."

"If I'd known what I was doing to you," Anna said deliberately, "I would have stopped."

Her words dropped into thick silence.

"The hell you would."

Anna closed her eyes briefly, and tried one more time. "I pulled you into this mess, but I didn't mean to. Blade, you don't have to—"

"Forget it. I don't want out."

Her eyes flung wide. "What?"

His words were flat with conviction. It seemed he was prepared to ignore the danger, ignore her psychic talent, but Anna couldn't let go of her wariness yet. "De Rocheford doesn't know you're involved. You could help me and still keep your distance from all of this."

"Seber may have ID'ed me. He saw the Jeep."

"In the dark. Briefly."

"The man's a professional."

Anna backed up a step, needing to be free of his touch, needing to think clearly. Blade wanted her now, maybe for longer, but that was no guarantee they would stay together. She'd had many bonds broken in her life. When her father had died, she had felt it, as if something had broken inside her. When her mother had died she hadn't felt that same immediacy, they had drifted too far apart, but she had known. She feared the breaking of this bond most of all. "I don't want you to become a target because of me."

"You want me to crawl under the bed and hide while de Rocheford does his best to kill you?"

His tone was incredulous, and she could see his thwarted male impatience, feel his need to assert dominance over her.

Abruptly, he turned, bracing his hands on the railing, looking into the rising sun as if he could pull answers from the burning spread of light. His back was broad and strong, deeply grooved, inflexible. The breeze disturbed his hair so that it drifted around his broad shoulders. He looked wild and grim, and she wondered that she had any control over him at all.

He would do what he wanted, regardless of her wishes. He would expose himself to danger to protect her. She felt both helpless and enraged, as protective as a tigress with a cub. For the first time in years she had someone to love, someone other than herself to protect, but trying to protect Blade was just another definition for impossible.

He turned, pinning her with his dark gaze. "I told you I just recently left the military," he said flatly. "I was in the Special Air Service for a number of years. It's not a generally known fact, because I went to a lot of trouble to keep it quiet. I've done stints with the British, Australian and New Zealand forces. In the past twelve years, I've seen a lot of bad situations, dealt with a lot of bad people. The reason I'm telling you this is that you have to trust me to take care of de Rocheford, because he's not just your problem, he's mine, too. I'm damn tired of watching you get hurt and not being able to do a thing to help."

His expression was set, his manner calm, as if all the decisions had been made. "It's taken me a long time to find you, and I was almost too late, but I've learned my lesson. Until this situation is resolved, you will stay in this suite and rest, because I need to know exactly where you are every second of the day. You will eat nice food, sleep as much as you want, order any damn thing you want from room service or the boutiques downstairs. When you need to go out, I'll be with you. I'm going to take care of de Rocheford and Seber. They are history. Believe it."

Anna stared at Blade in dazed disbelief. He had said de Rocheford was his problem, too, but that was only because she had inflicted visions on him. Visions that he didn't like or want. Now he was giving orders as if he were reading a grocery list and expecting her to obey. She'd already guessed he'd been in the special forces. It didn't take any stretch of the imagination to see him as an officer.

"You won't run anywhere ever again," he stated, as if she were dimwitted and needed to be told twice, that from now on, she would do everything he said.

"I won't run," she snapped. Why would she, she thought acidly, when she'd already figured out all by her little self that it was time to stop de Rocheford in his tracks? "Now, if you're finished…" she muttered, turning on her heel.

"I'm not." Blade cursed silently, his hand curling around her upper arm. He'd gone overboard, he knew it, but he'd been so furious that, even now, she was still trying to shut him out, trying to protect *him*. She had said she loved him. Her admission had taken him by surprise, knocked him off balance, and he was still reeling. De Rocheford had sent a hit man out to kill her, and she was worried about *his* safety.

A long, tense moment passed before she even acknowledged his hold. She turned her head, glanced at his hand and lifted a brow. "I thought you were supposed to be the last of the great lovers? I hope you haven't been paying too much attention to your press."

Blade jerked her towards him, at the same time stepping into her, so that she was off balance enough for him to slide his hands down the line of her back, over the firm curve of her bottom, then up beneath the shirt until his palms cupped naked flesh.

He heard her rough intake of air, felt the soft impact of her breasts before she braced her hands on his chest and shoved back a few inches. Her glare had turned intriguingly molten, and he stared into her eyes, bemused.

"What press?" he murmured, his heart pounding, every muscle in his body tightening in anticipation. He felt sharply alive and aroused, delighted by the fiery creature in his arms.

"I'm beginning to wonder myself." She glanced at the bulge that strained the front of his jeans, shoved bluntly against her hip. "The press that says you're the last of the great lovers."

Blade's delight smouldered into irritation. "Where in hell did you read that?"

"There was a magazine in the bathroom. There's a photo of you with some blonde in a skimpy dress. At least, I think it was a dress. There were so many holes in it, it was hard to tell."

He winced. Either his mother or his sister, Roma, would have left that the last time they visited. Or Aunt Sophie. Oh yeah, his money was definitely on Aunt Sophie. "I didn't touch her," he said bluntly.

Her eyes narrowed, and Blade's delight shuddered back to life: she was jealous.

"The article also said that you were the last of the great lovers," she continued in a clipped voice. "The tomcat to end all tomcats. Mothers should lock up their daughters, because no woman was safe from you. Maybe the blonde just slipped your mind."

"She didn't slip my mind," he said from between gritted teeth.

Anna pulled in a breath. She decided that for as long as she was with Blade, no other woman was getting within a mile of him. "You mean you remember them all?"

He cocked his head to one side, his regard watchful. "There weren't that many. Besides, she wasn't a red-head."

Anna wondered if she'd missed a vital piece of the conversation. "You only make love to redheads?"

"When I had the time. I went searching among the redheads. Of course, a lot of women colour their hair red, so that made for some confusion, but I got by."

According to the magazine article he'd done a lot more than just "get by." "Why redheads?"

He removed a hand from her butt and wound a finger in her hair, dangling a lock of it in front of her face. Morning sunlight shot red fire off the strands. "Guess."

A hot blush heated her cheeks, a shimmer of wonder threading the uncomfortable knowledge that other women had been this close to Blade, maybe even closer. And they'd probably known what they were do-ing in bed. She might not like his methods, but all those years when she'd thought she was alone, Blade had *searched* for her. "The dreams?"

"The dreams," he said. Then his mouth came down on hers.

When Blade finally came up for air, his head was spinning. It was only a few steps to the bed, but he was beginning to wonder if they were going to make it.

Anna swayed in his arms. "Is it true what the magazine said? About how good you are in bed?"

He swung her up into his arms. "I'll leave that for you to judge. You liked what I did to you before." He studied the curiosity in her eyes and felt the little shudder that ran through her. "There's more."

Her arms slid around his neck; he felt her fingers tangling in his hair. She buried her face against his bare shoulder as he strode back into the bedroom.

"How much more?"

Her fingers were stroking his scalp now, moving in a rhythmic way that made him want to purr with pleasure. He was hard, aching, he could hardly wait, but this time he would let her dictate the pace. There was a lot more for her to learn, and plenty of time to learn it. He didn't want to scare her any more than he already had her first time out.

"A lot more." He set her down on her feet beside the bed, shucked his jeans, then lay down, naked, on his back. He saw her blank look of surprise and grinned, propping his arms behind his head. "This time you get to be on top."

Chapter 12

Later that morning, Anna showered and dressed, slipping on her stained jeans with a grimace and tying the huge chambray shirt into a knot at her waist. When she walked out into the lounge, Blade was on the phone.

He set the receiver down and looked at her assessingly. "We need to get you some more clothes. A business suit, for starters. I'll get you some things from the boutique in the lobby; then we'll start making some calls. First the police, then your solicitor. I've organised Lombards' legal counsel to be present at both interviews."

He strolled over and kissed her, taking his time. "I've also organised a security guard for the door until I come back, but I shouldn't be more than a few minutes. Come and say hello to him before I leave. I've ordered breakfast. It should be up shortly."

Blade introduced her to the guard, Danny, then

pushed her back into the suite before telling her to lock up.

She wandered restlessly around the flat, pulling out books and reading the back cover copy, while she waited for Blade to come back. She idly checked his selection of music, and picked up his family photos to look at them.

The Lombards were a big family. There seemed to be a lot of children, a great many happy occasions, even though she knew they'd had their troubles.

There was a knock at the door. She used the peephole, saw a waiter with a breakfast trolley, recognised the security guy's sports jacket, the tag on his pocket, and opened the door so the trolley could be wheeled in.

The security man was different.

Anna frowned as he stepped forward, and then she saw the gun in his hand. She glanced around wildly. The waiter also had a gun. He was short and stocky. Seber.

"You've caused me a lot of trouble," he said.

She heard the other man move behind her. An arm came around her neck, a cloth was pressed to her mouth and nose, then everything went black.

Even before Blade opened the door to the suite, he knew something was wrong. Danny wasn't on duty.

His nostrils flared, testing the strange chemical scent on the air. "Anna!"

Panic punched hard at his gut. He dropped the bags of clothes and shoes and searched the apartment.

He found the security guard slumped unconscious on the floor in one of the bedrooms. He'd been hit on the head, but he was breathing, his pulse even. Anna's briefcase was sitting in her room where she'd left it, beside the bed.

Seconds later, Blade found the note that had been left on the dining table.

De Rocheford requested his presence for dinner tonight at his seaside estate, in order to discuss business. He had left a phone number.

De Rocheford had Anna. Fear and fury roared through Blade. Henry's nasty little pet, Seber, had walked in here, knocked out the security guard and taken her. Blade didn't know how it could have happened. His security people were hand-picked. They were good. Somehow, he had slipped up; he had made a mistake when he absolutely could not afford to make a mistake.

Blade went cold inside. He wasn't fooled into thinking de Rocheford was willing to negotiate. He knew how the game was played, probably better than de Rocheford did. Anna was alive, but only because she served a purpose—as bait. There was only one reason for this note. Henry, the optimistic son of a bitch, was planning to kill him as well.

He called the infirmary and ordered the duty nurse up to check over the guard. Then he stabbed in the number on the scrap of paper. De Rocheford answered on the first ring.

"Hurt her and I'll kill you," Blade said, low and cold, not bothering to identify himself.

"I don't know what you're talking about, Lombard," de Rocheford murmured. "I know you were in the military, but even so, that's very crude behaviour. Don't bother issuing any more threats, because they won't wash. My security is better than anything you bumbling military types are likely to come up with."

Blade's hand tightened on the receiver, almost snapping it in two. De Rocheford was obviously trying not to incriminate himself over the phone, just in case Blade was taping the conversation—which he was. It was a matter of family security that all Lombard family private telephone conversations were taped. The tapes were, for the most part, never listened to, and were constantly erased and taped over, because the purpose of the tapes was only for dangerous situations like this.

Henry's message was unmistakeable. He was armed, ready and waiting. "I'll be at your gate at eight o'clock," Blade bit out. "You'd better have Anna with you."

"That would be impossible," he said smoothly, "since my stepdaughter has been missing, presumed dead, for seven years. And, Lombard…"

Blade didn't answer, just waited.

"Do come alone. The invitation is only for one. I'm sure you understand."

Blade let the receiver click back into place before he lost his cool completely. He had wanted to reach down the phone, wrap his fingers around Henry's artificially tanned throat and strangle the little weasel. For a moment he entertained the vision, and then reality struck, almost sending him to his knees.

Anna.

He caught the back of a couch with both hands, head bowed, fingers sinking into supple leather, while he fought back a sickening whirl of panic and fear.

Sweet Mother of God, he couldn't lose her.

His head came up, nostrils flaring once more as he caught the faint chemical residue lingering in the air.

The bastards had drugged her. His eyes squeezed shut, every muscle in his body locking tight on a flood of raw rage at what had been done to a woman who was so sensitive she could *feel* anger.

A tap at the door snapped him back to the present. He let in the nurse, and the two burly members of the cleaning staff she'd commandeered to carry the stretcher. The security guard was examined, then removed to the infirmary for observation and examination by a doctor.

Blade shut the door behind them. Minutes later, he found himself kneeling on his unmade bed, the pillow Anna had slept on in his hands. He couldn't remember getting there. He shook his head, dazed, his fingers tightening their hold. He wanted to hold Anna, to wrap her close and bury his face in her hair, breathe in her scent, to simply have her close.

Images of the past night seared across his mind, along with other, older images, drenched with violence and fear. Every time Anna had been in trouble, she had called out to him. She hadn't been able to this time, because they had surprised her, drugged her.

The pillow dropped from his fingers, forgotten, as a compulsion as familiar as the dreams and visions drew him out to the terrace, outside, beneath the endless expanse of the sky, where anything seemed possible. He gripped the railing, oblivious to the warm pleasure of the sunlight, the drifting breeze feathering his skin. When the drug wore off, Anna would call out to him, and he would find her.

The psychic link was no longer an intrusion. He

wanted it. The silent, uncanny communication was *theirs,* a link that had bound them together for more than half his life.

In the meantime, he would make his own preparations.

Anna was being held hostage. Getting her back would take all his skill, all his control and discipline. He was going to need help.

As much as he would have liked to storm de Rocheford's bolt-hole and beat the living daylights out of him, he knew he wasn't going to get the chance and grimly accepted the loss. Anna would have to be snatched from beneath de Rocheford's nose, quickly and quietly. If Henry became suspicious at any point, he would simply have her killed.

Blade walked back inside and once more picked up the phone.

Ben McCabe arrived first, followed half an hour later by Gabriel West and Carter Rawlings.

When they were all assembled, Blade briefly surveyed the three tanned, muscular men sprawled like young lions on various chairs and couches. Ben and Carter were both fresh in from an overseas trip. Their jaws were darkly stubbled, hair grown to shaggy manes, Ben's as dark as Blade's own, Carter's light hair streaked a startling silver by a hot tropical sun. West had been living in Auckland for the past couple of months while he ran a sniper training course. He was quiet, as always, his deceptively sleepy amber gaze focused on Blade.

Blade outlined the situation. "If you can't help me, I'll understand," he said quietly. "I don't plan to go through any official channels—there isn't time—and besides, de Rocheford has his sticky fingers in too many political pies. Even if we could get a police team in there, there's a big risk that he'll have some kind of advance warning. He said his security is good, and I believe him."

Ben, who had taken up pacing with the kind of restless, coiled energy of someone still wired for combat, unable yet to fully adjust to the civilised confines of a city apartment, halted near the patio door and turned his intense blue gaze on Blade. "Who did you say this woman is?"

"Anna Tarrant." Blade pulled the pile of newspaper clippings from Anna's briefcase and let them drop on the coffee table.

Carter cleared his throat. West studied his boots for an inordinate period of time.

Ben was very still. "The dead heiress?"

"She's not dead."

"You sure about that?"

Blade reined in his temper. "Positive."

Blade could feel the weight of their combined disbelief warring with their rock-steady trust in him. He had trained and fought with these men, served as their commanding officer. They were closer than friends—they were family. And he had never needed them more.

Carter broke the silence. "Oh, jeez," he groaned. "You're sleeping with her."

Carter's tacit acceptance of everything Blade had said eased the sudden thick tension; then Carter's words registered on Blade.

"I am not *sleeping* with her," he got out from between clenched teeth, wondering what it was about him that made people instantly assume that if he spent time with a woman, he was sleeping with her. "She's not…casual."

West crossed his arms over his chest. "He's in love with her."

Blade cast him an annoyed glance. "I am not *in love*."

In love was a weak, wimpy term to describe the violence of his emotions. Right now there was nothing soft or gentle in him. He wanted Anna back, and he wanted to kill de Rocheford.

Carter's eyes narrowed speculatively on the newspaper clippings. "Pretty girl," he murmured, "but she's not your usual type. A bit on the thin side. So, when this is over you won't mind if I—"

Blade snatched the clipping from Carter's hands. "What is this with 'my usual type'?" he growled softly. "Touch her, Rawlings, and you're a dead man."

West picked up Anna's passport and studied the colour photo. "She's a redhead."

Blade met West's knowing gaze. West never said much—he gave new meaning to the term "the strong, silent type"—but he tended to notice things that most people missed. Blade wondered what else he had noticed. He didn't have long to wait.

"She's the one you've been looking for," West added softly.

"I'm going to marry her," Blade stated, his flat certainty sending another minor shockwave through the room.

Ben dropped back into his chair. He reached for one of the newspaper clippings. It showed Anna Tarrant as a child no older than Ben's daughter, Bunny, her dark hair tied in pigtails, eyes large and solemn in her little-girl face. "She's been missing for years. Where's she been all this time?"

"Running."

Ben replaced the cutting very gently. The blue of his eyes was fierce and cold. "Then let's get her away from the bastard. We need a plan, and we need equipment. De Rocheford isn't short of cash. He'll have sophisticated security and some major firepower backing him."

"He's hired an out-of-work mercenary."

Ben eyed him piercingly. "Who?"

"Eric Seber. Gray sent a file on him this morning. Seber's been on the mercenary circuit for nearly five years. Before that he was a cop."

Ben smiled grimly. "I've heard of him. He's a methodical bastard, but not top line. De Rocheford shouldn't have skimped. If he wanted to win, he should have paid for the best."

Blade smiled coldly. "He probably thinks he did."

Chapter 13

A choking sensation jerked Anna from unconsciousness. Henry was leaning over her, a satisfied smirk on his face.

Sunlight shafted into the room, the angle of it denoting late afternoon. She'd been out for most of the day, and she was still woozy and faintly nauseous from whatever drug they had used. There was a bitter taste in her mouth, the sensation that something small and hard was stuck in her throat.

She suddenly knew why Henry looked so smug; he had just fed her something.

"What did you give me?" Her throat was so dry the demand came out as a thready whisper.

"Just a couple of sleeping pills. They should keep you nicely knocked out."

He was as matter-of-fact and professional as a doctor leaning over a patient. She gagged, trying to roll on to her side to spit the residue of the pills out. Henry's hands came down hard on her shoulders, pinning her to the floor. She felt dopey already, heavy and lethargic. He was enjoying her pathetic attempt to struggle.

Rage and fear gathered into a tight, hard knot inside her. "Why are you doing this?" she demanded. "It can't be for the money. You always had plenty of that."

Henry eyed her with cold, analytical interest, as if he was examining an insect beneath a microscope. "Clever girl. Money was never an issue. My stepfather and your father were always very generous."

"Did you kill my father?" She had never before voiced her suspicion, but now it seemed entirely probable that he *had* killed Hugh Tarrant.

"Tut-tut. He died in an accident."

"But once he was out of the way, you decided Tarrants should be yours. You tried to kill me, and you killed my mother."

Henry's grip tightened on her shoulders. "Eloise was already a hypochondriac. She took so many different drugs it was a wonder she didn't kill herself." He smiled, but his eyes stayed empty. "She depended on sleeping pills. I gave her the same ones I just made you swallow. Killing Eloise was easy."

Anna had a flash of memory. Eloise always vague and distant, dreamy, from the medication she couldn't get through the day without. It had torn her in two to leave her mother behind when she'd made the decision to run, but she had known she couldn't keep both of them hidden. Eloise had never worked a day in her life. She had needed someone to keep an eye on her through the day. Otherwise she did silly, muddled things, like leave appliances going.

She'd been beautiful and harmless, and she wouldn't have hurt a fly. Anna stared into Henry's remorseless gaze and saw the familiar shift in his eyes—the dreamy warmth that lived in her nightmares, the secret he'd tried to share with her—felt all the hairs at the base of her neck stand on end as he lifted a hand to her cheek. The back of his fingers stroked against her skin. She flinched, rage and fury flashing through her. She wanted to hit him, swing at him with her fists, but she could barely move her arms. If she had a gun she'd shoot him. She could feel his intent, the knowledge that Henry had never wanted to just kill her—feel the weight of what he wanted crawling on her skin, pressing against her temples. He'd never managed to get beyond this, a touch on her cheek, she'd always gotten away from him. Panic spiraled through her because she knew she wasn't going to get away from him this time. She was trapped. She could feel the sleeping pills dragging her down, and something hot and desperate leaped to life inside her, a wild surge of impotent rage, choking in her throat, bursting outward on a raw cry of denial. *"No!"*

Henry reeled back as if she'd struck him, clutching at his head. "What did you do?" he demanded in a curiously high-pitched voice.

It took Anna a dazed moment to identify the pitch as panic.

"What did you do?" he roared.

Anna stared at him blankly. What had she done?

She had lost her temper, fury and grief exploding outward. She had looked at Henry and shouted "No."

"Witch," he muttered. "You're a damn witch like your mother."

Witch. Her stomach twisted, and she lurched to her knees, swaying. This time Henry did nothing to stop her.

What had she done? She struggled to analyse what had happened. She must have used her mind in some way—hit out with her mind. It had been a knee-jerk reaction, an unequivocal rejection of evil.

It was the same thing she did to Blade, but in reverse. Striking out instead of calling.

Henry backed up to the door and rapped on it, his gaze locked on her, a little wild, as if she'd just grown fangs and was liable to bite. Immediately Anna heard the scrape of a bolt being pulled back; then Seber appeared, peering over Henry's shoulder with horrified interest, as if he'd been listening at the door and now wanted to see the monster for real.

"I always knew you were strange," Henry snapped, cold loathing in his voice as he backed from the room. "But that won't help you in a few hours."

Blade let Ben and Carter into the suite. It was late afternoon, and they were almost ready to go.

Minutes later there was a knock at the door. Ben let West in. There was a brief, stunned silence. West had always had an edgy style with clothes, but today he'd surpassed himself. He was dressed all in black, which was no big surprise, since they had all agreed to wear black street clothes, with nothing identifiably military on them, in case they were compromised. Over his, West wore a long, elegant duster coat. His hair had grown long enough that it tumbled to his shoulders in dark, silky ringlets. In stark contrast to his almost feminine hair, his jaw was square and stubbled, his eyes amber and unblinking beneath straight, dark brows. He looked like a poster boy for the mob. He had more coats draped over one arm.

Blade whistled his appreciation. "What happened to you? The fashion police give you a makeover?"

West's tawny eyes glinted with amusement. He opened the coat, displaying the arsenal beneath. A shoulder holster housed what Blade knew to be West's favourite hand gun—a Bernadelli Practical, a custom-made sporting pistol, exquisitely balanced and adapted for street use. Blade knew for a fact that West always carried a knife strapped to his ankle, and sometimes one in a spine sheath. He probably had a back-up gun strapped to his other ankle, as well. West had spent time on the streets as a kid. He didn't say much about that time, but they all understood. Some children clung to a blanket or a cuddly toy; West had gone for hardware. It was a security thing.

Blade eyed him steadily. "You can't take the guns."

"Don't worry, I'll leave them behind, but it'll be like going out naked," West said dryly, tossing a coat to each of them. "Consider these early Christmas presents. Did a favour for a friend, and he insisted on paying me. Got half a dozen of the damn things."

Blade shrugged into the coat and caught a glimpse of his reflection in a full-length mirror near the door. Oh, yeah, the archangel from hell. Now he looked dangerous. "What did your friend do, work on a movie set?"

"Close. He's a men's wear retailer. Got in the way of some Asian bad guys."

"Triad?"

West shook his head, wandering over to the dining table where Blade had spread out maps. "If it was Triad, he wouldn't still be alive."

They all gravitated to the table and began finalising their plans. De Rocheford was expecting a land assault. They had decided to go in by sea. That afternoon, Blade had chartered a flight, and West had done a reconnaisance of the property by air at a high enough altitude to avoid suspicion, using some of the cutting-edge camera equipment he owned. West was a technology buff and a perfectionist. The result of his expertise was a set of high-resolution photographs, displaying de Rocheford's peninsula in exquisite detail.

Carter studied the shots that showed the cliffs to best advantage. It was his job to choose their insertion point, because where they beached depended on where the most accessible route up the cliff face lay. They were all competent rock climbers, but Carter was extraordinary. He had spent a lot of his leisure time either scaling mountains or crawling through caves, potholing, and had a feel for climbing—a canny knack of finding footholds or handholds where there seemed to be none. He drew an arrow on one photograph, then pulled a map toward him and made a corresponding mark on it. He flicked a glance at Blade. "You've got confirmation our lady's there?"

Blade bit back his frustration. Hours had passed, and he didn't have confirmation. The plain fact was, Anna could be anywhere. He had been banking on her mentally contacting him, but so far, he'd had sweet nothing.

"We assume she's there," he said flatly. "We don't have another lead, and de Rocheford is just cocky

enough to want to flaunt his power. He's spent a fortune on security and buying toy soldiers. I'm betting
he wants to play with them.''

He leaned over Carter's shoulder, studying the place
he'd picked out as a landing site. ''I'm also priming
the cops to search his place tonight. Ray Cornell's been
on Seber's tail for weeks, trying to catch him with his
pants down. I told him I could have an address for him
tonight, in which case the police will be knocking on
the front door, creating a diversion, while we go in the
back way. But I'm putting that decision to the vote. I
won't call Ray unless you all agree.''

Ben asked several curt questions, and they tossed the
matter back and forth for a few minutes.

They had already discussed all the reasons why they
couldn't take firearms with them. They were all SAS—
Blade knew that even though he had left just months
ago, he would still be tagged as such. If they were
caught carrying out a hostage rescue mission on home
territory, the salsa would hit the fan. Ben, Carter and
West would be kicked out of the Service, and they
would all bring the SAS into disrepute. If they were
found to be carrying firearms, they could face criminal
charges, as well. In any case, this whole mission hinged
on getting in and out quickly and quietly, not tearing
the place apart with HK submachine guns. Adding the
police to the mix both gave them an advantage and put
them at more risk.

''It's called hedging our bets,'' Blade said. ''De
Rocheford thinks he's got all his ducks in a row, but
he's forgotten one thing. The good guys only play by
the bad guy's rules in the movies.''

''Uh-huh,'' Carter said reflectively. ''So the rules of

engagement are that we're gonna have the bad guys *and* the cops after our hides.'' He shook his head in admiration. ''It was just as well you left the SAS when you did; otherwise, they would have promoted you.''

Half an hour later, they stepped out of the elevator.

Sadie Carson, a brisk, fifty-something woman with a boyish haircut and trim jeans, was waiting to get on with a trolley of plants. She and her twin sister Addie were on the staff of Lombards and took care of all the hotel's plants and gardens. Now Sadie took her time giving them all an unabashed once-over.

She had got to know them all last year when they had based an operation to catch a terrorist at the old Pacific Royal hotel, which had since been demolished. She treated them all like slightly dim nephews, but she always made no bones about enjoying the view.

''Nice earring,'' she commented, leaning forward to peer at the small gem winking at Blade's lobe. ''Got one just like it.''

Blade's brows went up. He'd left his hair loose, and the earring in, though normally he didn't wear it when he was ''working.'' But in this case, the black balaclava would cover it.

She nodded sagely, hands on hips. ''You boys off on a mission?''

West cleared his throat, his eyes wary. ''What makes you say that?''

Sadie gave him a pitying look. ''I can smell the gun oil. But those coats do a good job of hiding the weaponry. You boys should get yourselves some sunglasses. You'd look just like that movie *Matrix*.''

With a cheerful nod, she pushed her trolley into the

elevator, a pair of gardening gloves flopping from a back jeans' pocket. The elevator doors swished closed.

Ben traded a glance with Blade as they strode through the car park. "Ever thought of putting Sadie in charge of security?"

"Nah," Carter said, before Blade could reply. "Too scary. Just imagine the pat downs."

Chapter 14

The door slammed behind Henry and Seber. Anna heard a key turn, the bolt rammed home.

She listened for their retreating footsteps, then fell forward on her hands and knees, retching. The pill that had been lodged in her throat shot out, but the other one must have gone all the way down.

Sitting back on her feet, she shakily wiped her mouth and stared around the small room she'd been shoved into. The sun was setting, and panic gripped her; she had to wonder if this was the last daylight she would ever see. The only window was barred but had no glass in it. She could feel the brisk sea breeze on her face, and she lurched to her feet and stumbled forward, grasping the bars, pressing against them as if she could magically slide between the columns of cold metal.

The view was familiar.

She blinked, for a moment disbelieving; then the

truth hit. She was locked in what was left of the old beach house on the cliffs near Henry's modern, architecturally designed eyrie.

The house was in reality a dilapidated old farmhouse, the original home on the property Henry had bought years ago when he had insisted they all move to New Zealand. They had never actually lived here, because the new house had been completed and ready for them.

Anna had always thought of this entire property as belonging solely to Henry, even though it had been bought with Tarrant money. It had certainly never belonged to either Anna or her mother. It was built at the tip of a wild peninsula and was as isolated as a fortress, guarded on three sides by the broken cliffs that plunged down to rocky beaches below, protected on the fourth by high fences and a heavy-gauge steel, electronically controlled gate. She had no doubt the security here was even more impressive now than it had been when she left. Keeping up with the latest security gizmos had always been a particular hobby of Henry's.

Her fingers tightened with bruising force on the bars. The last time she had been in this house, she had nearly died.

She had been a teenager and had sneaked away to spend the night huddled on one of the old beds that used to reside in the bedrooms, and had woken to find the room ablaze and thick with black smoke. She had escaped by breaking a window that had been mysteriously nailed down, but it had been a near thing.

Anna remained standing for as long as she was able, fighting the effects of the sleeping pill, staring through the bars at the vast expanse of the sea, watching dusk deepen and the ripe, golden orb of a full moon crest the horizon. Her mind was muddled, hazy, but her dilemma was not—she could call out to Blade, but she hesitated. Maybe he could find her in time, get past Henry's security and help her, but in doing so, she would draw him into danger and possibly cause his death.

When she could no longer stand, she knelt, clutching the windowsill until her fingers went numb with the effort of keeping herself upright.

When she fell for the third time, she decided to stay on the floor and put all her remaining energy into mentally fighting the drugging effect of the pill.

Unfortunately, that strategy wasn't working any better than the first one had. The scents of dust and mould and the mice that inhabited the cottage were acrid in her nostrils. She hated the smell, hated the knowledge that she was lying in utter filth and didn't have the energy to even lift her cheek from the gritty surface of the bare wood floor.

An argument broke out in the adjoining room. She could hear Henry's smooth voice, then the flatter, more staccato cadence of Seber's. Occasionally a third man interjected.

Blade's name jerked her back to full consciousness on a hot pump of adrenalin.

Her eyes popped open. She had wondered why they had bothered with the sleeping pills when Seber could simply have shot her. They could have tossed her body into a boat, taken her miles offshore and dumped her by now, but they hadn't.

She could have kicked herself. The chance that they didn't know Blade was helping her had always been slim, but she'd had to consider it, despite the fact that they had taken her from the Lombard Hotel. Henry had known all along that Blade was helping her, and he was planning to kill him, too. They were drawing him into a trap, using her as bait.

She had to call out to him, give him as much information as she could on her location. She didn't know if it would help, but she had to try to warn him.

She pushed herself to her knees, then grabbed for the bars, finding them and dragging herself upright. She swayed, propping her weight against the wall, her face pressed into the bars as she concentrated on remaining upright and keeping her grip.

She stared fiercely at the sea. Now that she had to do this for real, *knowing* what she was doing, she was struck with the fear that it wouldn't work. Closing her eyes, she concentrated, searching for that inner place. Blade's face wavered, his expression grim, dark eyes fixed piercingly on her. He said her name, an impression of sound and heat washed through her in a glittering torrent. For the barest moment she thought she caught the scent of him, felt a familiar jolt as if he'd reached out across the distance that separated them and touched her.

Tears shivered on her lashes, the hot spill quickly turned cold. She had to wonder if that was the last time she would ever see him, then she was slipping down, down, and once again everything went black.

Blade stared at Ben, once more becoming aware that he was standing beside the Jeep, his hand braced against cold metal. Sensation crowded in on him as abruptly as if someone had just flicked a switch: the cool rush of the sea breeze against his skin, in his hair, laced with the scents of salt and dried kelp; the rhythmic wash of the waves. Ben's hand was gripping his arm, steadying him. He could hear the faint noises West and Carter made as they pulled the inflatable boat off the back of Carter's truck.

Ben released his grip. "What is it?" he demanded. "You look like you saw a ghost."

"Not a ghost." Blade shook free of the stark image of Anna's hands clenched around bars, the sea shimmering beneath moonlight. The view had been up high, as if the building was perched on a cliff. That described de Rocheford's place.

Rage and relief twisted through him, mixed with a grim satisfaction. Anna had called out to him, and she'd done her best to show him where she was. She was all right, but someone had put her in a damn cage.

The strangeness of the communication barely registered. He had been going crazy waiting, and his primary feeling was relief. A part of him still wanted logical answers, but the important thing had been that the communication link had worked.

Blade pulled out his mobile phone and punched in a number.

Ray picked up on the first ring. "If you can tell me where Seber is, I'll name my fourth-born child after you," he muttered. "We got a paint scraping from Seber's car, tying him to a hit-and-run, and now the bastard's dropped out of sight. Every cop in the damn city's looking for him."

"I've got the address for you."

Ray noted the address. "De Rocheford. Are you

sure? This guy practically bankrolls every charity there
is, including the police widows and orphans fund.''

Blade told him in cold detail exactly why he should
search de Rocheford's estate. He saved the piece of
information he knew would enrage Ray the most for
last. ''Seber used a police ID to get past my security
in the hotel.''

Ray used a succinct Anglo-Saxon word. ''You've
got proof of that?''

''One of the hidden security cameras we've recently
installed caught him entering the building by a back
entrance. The guard he knocked out can testify that
Seber presented police ID.''

''Not so smart after all,'' Ray said with satisfaction.
''The Tarrant heiress, you say?'' His tone turned
thoughtful. ''Eloise Tarrant died of an overdose a few
months ago. There was a big funeral—hit the front
page of all the papers. The hit-and-run we've just tied
Seber to is the Tarrants' solicitor, Emerson Stevens,
who was killed just weeks ago. I've still got the file on
my desk. I guess with the Tarrant women out of the
way, that leaves de Rocheford all by himself in the
driver's seat.''

''Except for Anna,'' Blade said flatly. ''If you want
Seber, be at de Rocheford's estate at eight sharp, tonight. He's armed and dangerous, and he won't be
alone. Bring some backup you can trust.''

''Where will you be?''

Blade smiled grimly at the suspicion in Ray's voice.
''You won't see us.''

''Damn, you didn't give me much notice.'' Ray
swore softly. ''But then, you planned it that way.
You're already there, ready to go in. Who are you tak-

ing with you? Wait, don't answer that, let me guess. McCabe, Carter Rawlings. Gabriel West—I heard he's been in town lately. A damn Pagoda squad.''

Blade didn't confirm or deny. The title Pagoda squad invoked a certain mystique. It was in-house jargon for a category certain highly trained SAS teams had been classified under years ago—unofficially, of course, because these guys weren't supposed to exist—and was now a metaphor for a team that was so tight its members fought, moved and thought virtually as a single entity.

Blade waited patiently while Ray considered what they were going to do. Ray had done undercover operations for the SAS and understood exactly what they were trying to achieve: a sneak and snatch. He also knew that a police team that was forced to go through official channels might be too late to save Anna.

When he spoke, his voice was cold with warning. "I didn't hear any of this, but just in case you're anywhere near de Rocheford's estate tonight, don't go in there armed. If I find any weapons on you, I'll have to bust all your asses. This is civilian territory, not a war zone.''

"We're just planning on doing a little night fishing out that way. The only thing we'll be armed with are fishing knives. But if you're worried about your career path,'' he added softly, "don't shine any spotlights over the cliffs.''

Blade terminated the call on Ray's short, hard oath.

Ben lifted the outboard from the rear of the vehicle. "Do you think he'll do it?''

"He'll do it.'' Blade snagged a large canvas duffel

filled with rope and abseiling equipment. "He won't like it, but he'll do it."

Anna awoke, curled on the floor of the old house. She dragged herself upright, brushed tangled hair from her face and checked her watch, seeing with relief that little more than an hour had passed. She must have spat out more of the second sleeping pill than she'd thought.

It was fully dark now, condensation hung cool and heavy in the air, the smell of mice and dust was over-laid by the faint sweetness of the honeysuckle that grew in a rampant tangle outside the window.

For the first time, she took stock of her surroundings. She was in the storeroom, a lean-to that had been built on one side of the house. After the fire had swept through, what was left of the old farmhouse had been left to rot, but the lean-to had been a more recent, stur-dier addition, and hadn't been touched by the blaze. When Henry had fortified the room to hold her, he had simply put bars on the single window and ripped the shelving off the walls, leaving the room as bare as a cell. There was nothing she could use as a tool to try to free herself, nothing she could use as a weapon. The best she could hope for was to create a diversion so she could try to escape.

Of course, she didn't hold out much hope that a di-version would save her, either. She was still drowsy, her limbs clumsy and leaden, and Seber had a gun. No matter how fast she ran, she couldn't outrun a bullet.

Chapter 15

The inflatable nudged the beach. The four men flowed out, secured the boat, and began moving up the broken rocky face that led to the top of the cliff. They were dressed completely in black, wearing Kevlar vests—courtesy of one of Gray Lombard's manufacturing contacts—with the addition of blunt trauma shields beneath to absorb the shock of an incoming round in the event they were fired upon.

The body armour was heavy, and they were all sweating, but no one complained. They weren't taking firearms, but damned if they would die from getting shot. The parts of their faces not covered by balaclavas were smeared with camouflage paint. They had voice-activated radio headsets with lip microphones, and state-of-the-art night-vision gear, which at present they didn't need, because the moonlight was so bright. Their hands were bare for climbing, but when they reached the cliff top they would immediately pull on black, thin-skinned leather gloves to reduce the risk of naked skin reflecting light. The only weapons they carried were fighting knives sheathed in matt black pouches, again so as not to reflect light.

There would be no fingerprints, no gunfire, no trace of their presence when they left, except the rope they would leave behind. They would be in and out of the fortress estate before de Rocheford realised they had even been there.

Carter went first, moving with fluid ease. Blade followed, then McCabe, with West bringing up the rear. When they reached the edge of the cliff, they anchored the rope they would use for the descent by securing it around the trunk of one of the gnarled pohutukawa trees that fringed, and in some places grew down, the cliff face.

West took point. He had a sniper's patience and a hunter's uncanny awareness for what moved and *how* it should move. If de Rocheford had men patrolling this close to his house, West would spot them.

Minutes later, they were at the house. Ben went to work on the alarm system, stripping wires, attaching connectors, quickly bringing up the main menu on his laptop. He had the system neutralised in seconds. De Rocheford had made the basic mistake of spending big bucks on his main gate security and had left his back door standing wide open. His laxness was perfectly understandable, of course; it wasn't every day that a sea assault was mounted on a private residence.

They ghosted through the house, searching with silent efficiency. There was a couple watching television in a back apartment, the housekeeper and the gardener.

They left them undisturbed. By the time they reached the second floor, Blade knew the main part of the house was empty. He hadn't found Anna, and he hadn't found a room with bars in the window. He stared out of a window, adrenaline pumping, his gut knotting because he *knew* she was near, eyes raking the manicured grounds. Nothing about the view from these windows tallied with what Anna had shown him. It was all trees and lawn, the sea a more distant component.

There had been no sign of de Rocheford. They hadn't known whether he would be in the house or not. His absence probably meant he was down at the gate-house, where his main security system was installed—a small bunker housing an ultra-modern system that incorporated video cameras, electronics, spotlights and a sophisticated series of lasers, which must have driven the security guard crazy every time a small animal tripped one.

The shape of a roof further along the cliff caught Blade's eye. On the aerial photos there had been an overgrown ruin of a house, and it was a lot closer to the sea than this one was.

Anna crouched in the deep well of darkness by the storeroom door, ignoring the ache of muscles frozen too long in one position, back braced against the rough chill of the wall. She was awake and alert now—the cold had taken care of that.

She shivered and wrapped her arms around her middle, hugging Blade's shirt close against her body in a hopeless attempt to warm herself, her heart squeezing tight when she caught a faint whiff of his scent drifting up from the folds.

Blade would be on his way to rescue her, maybe even here by now, and he would be walking into a trap. Anger ignited like a hot flame, steadily feeding her fury as she doggedly watched the darker patch she knew was the door. She didn't know what she could do to help Blade, but she had to try.

How long before someone came to check on her? And when they did, would she be able to take them by surprise?

Long minutes passed. The moonlight gradually seeped from the room, until there was only a single thin beam slanting through the window. She caught the faint vibration of footsteps—not the heavy, deliberate tread of Seber—then the metallic scrape of the bolt. The door opened no more than a few inches, so little that she strained to see, not sure if her eyes were playing tricks on her. She waited, senses painfully alert for the preternatural jolt that signalled danger, but there was no prickling at the base of her neck, no kick of alarm deep in her stomach. Anna tensed, confused. She *knew* someone was there.

The darkness abruptly became darker, and she realised she was staring at the shadowy outline of a man. Someone had slipped into the room, moving without sound. The door softly closed.

His head turned toward her. The thin shaft of moonlight passed across a face that was blank shadow except for the cold glitter of his eyes. An executioner's face, hooded and formidable. Something else glinted, a knife, appearing in his hand as if by magic, although he had probably been gripping it when he entered the room.

So this is how it feels to die, she thought blankly,

launching herself at his legs. No great surge of adrenalin, no wrenching sadness or regret, just…nothing.

Her shoulder caught him at mid-thigh. Pain exploded all down one side. The man grunted, reeling off balance, and the odd disconnected feeling shattered as she landed heavily on her hands and knees. Anna launched herself at the door and wrenched it wide. Her right shoulder was numb, her arm and hand slow and clumsy, and as she lunged into the inky black opening she knew was the corridor, she cursed herself for not thinking to use her *left* shoulder as a battering ram.

A powerful hand landed at her nape, grabbing a fist full of hair and shirt, jerking her to a halt. A leather-clad hand clamped over her mouth, muffling the small panicked cry that exploded up from deep in her belly. His arm snaked around her waist, yanking her up and back against a hard, muscled body, so that her feet were left dangling.

His hold was so tight on her mouth and jaw that she was forced to breathe through her nose. Her nostrils flared as she fought to draw in enough oxygen to satisfy the pounding of her heart, the burning ache in her lungs, and as abruptly as if some internal switch had been flipped, she knew who her attacker was. As always, Blade's heat startled her; he seemed to hum with energy. She sagged in his hold, enduring the almost electrical tingle that just touching him engendered.

His grip on her mouth loosened fractionally. "It's okay, baby," he soothed, his voice a bare whisper, the tone lulling, as if he thought she might not be in a state to comprehend words. "It's me, Blade, and I've come to take you out of here. You don't have to fight anymore. I'm going to take my hand off your mouth in about two seconds, and when I do, I want you to be as quiet as you can. Nod your head if you understand.''

Anna moved her head the fraction of an inch his hold allowed.

His gloved hand slipped away. He set her back on her feet, his arm still around her waist, holding her against him. He bent and whispered against her ear, his voice slightly muffled by what she now realised was a balaclava.

''Don't talk at all until we're out of here. Follow directly behind me, and be careful where you step, there's a lot of debris on the floor. Do everything I tell you, *when* I tell you.''

She nodded again. His arm tightened in encouragement, and then she was free. She followed as he moved ahead of her down the short corridor. He was almost disappearing in front of her eyes, as she strained to see him, even though she knew he was only a step away. They passed through a doorway into what used to be the sitting room. Here, the gutted ruin of the old house was lit by moonlight filtering through holes that used to be windows. She stepped carefully, trying to emulate Blade's eerie silence. He paused beside a long shape on the floor and took her hand, his leather glove warm and smooth against her skin as he led her around what she realised was the crumpled body of a man.

Blade still had hold of her hand. He stopped, his head cocked; then he bent to whisper in her ear again. ''Someone's coming.''

He pulled her into the remains of the kitchen, positioning her in the darkest corner. The rest of the room was frighteningly light in contrast, dappled with silvery moonlight where pieces of the roof had fallen in. Blade placed himself directly in front of her, his big body completely obscuring hers, she realised, so that anyone looking in would see only him. He was dressed completely in black, more like a moving shadow than a man, but her breath dammed in her throat at the risk he was taking.

Seconds ticked by. Her face was pressed against Blade's back, which felt bulky and hard, and she realised he was wearing some kind of protective vest. But even so, heat radiated from him, instantly penetrating the layers of her clothing and making her aware of how cold she'd become sitting in that bleak room. She shivered in reflex but resisted the urge to crowd closer still, unwilling to do one thing to disturb his concentration.

Her nostrils filled with his scent every time she drew a breath, and as it had when she'd caught his scent from hugging his shirt, her heart squeezed with painful delight. She had thought she would never see him again. He smelled hot and sweaty and delicious, faintly briny, as if he'd been splashed with seawater. She felt the brush of his hand against her thigh, looked down and realised he still had the wicked-looking knife in his hand and was holding it partially behind him, presumably to stop any light from gleaming off it. She wondered why he didn't have a gun.

Footsteps sounded. Seber. Anna couldn't see him, but she easily identified his tread. Tension grabbed her stomach tight. Their hiding place was no more than a dark corner. All Seber had to do was look, yet Blade remained utterly motionless. He was as steady as a rock, the rhythm of his breathing unchanging as he stood in front of her, using his body as a living shield to protect her. If Seber shot at them, Blade could be killed, despite the protective vest.

A violent oath erupted from the storeroom, a loud bang, as if Seber had kicked a door against the wall in fury, then lower sounds, as he talked into a radio or a telephone. She could hear doors opening and closing and that deliberate tread. He was searching the house now, room by room.

Blade moved, his hand once more banded around her wrist, keeping her close as they picked their way around fallen timber and drifts of leaves. A gaping hole loomed, as if some giant creature had ripped away a whole section of wall.

He vaulted soundlessly down onto the ground, then reached up and lifted her, his hands warm at her waist. Immediately, dark figures detached themselves from the shadows.

Blade's hand once again clamped over her mouth, anticipating her startled gasp. ''They're with me,'' he whispered.

His hand clasped hers, and she was pulled along with him as the group closed around them, holding her in the centre. It was like being held in protective custody by a pack of half-wild panthers, and they didn't relax their vigilance, even when they reached the cliff's edge, fanning out in an arc and crouching down low, so that they were invisible unless someone stumbled right over them.

Blade pulled his balaclava off, shoving it into a pouch, which was attached to some kind of webbing. His face still looked wrong, and she realised it was streaked with camouflage paint. He grabbed a harness, which was laid out on the ground, and began explaining what they were going to do.

"This is modified abseiling gear," he said in a low voice as he clipped them both into a double harness. He showed her a small ratchet device. "This is a descendeur. It controls the rate of descent. If we slip, it'll stop us falling. Don't worry, we won't be abseiling— the cliff isn't vertical. This gear is just going to help us get down quickly and safely. All you have to do is use your hands and feet to steady you as we go down, I'll do the rest."

He clipped the descendeur onto another rope, which one of the men had readied, pulled it taut and stepped back over the edge. Anna felt a moment of stark disbelief as she was drawn back with Blade, then she was over the edge with him, her hands gripping the long grass and the rough broken rocks as they began the descent.

The wind had strengthened, blowing directly into the cliffs, blowing her loose hair wildly about her face. Blade and the harness provided some protection, but she couldn't prevent the shivers that racked her. He hovered protectively behind her, letting her take her time, encouraging her when she hesitated, calling her "sweetheart" and "baby."

Blade kept his mind fixed on their descent. The rock was sedimentary and treacherously crumbly. Centuries of being battered by sea winds had further weakened the already soft structure. They were going down fast, but still, they had to negotiate their way down at a slight angle.

Strangely enough, given that they had faced an armed force, the cliff was the part where it was most likely one of them would be hurt. Aside from the problem of finding out exactly where Anna was being held, they had achieved the rest of the mission with relative ease. None of de Rocheford's men had seen them, not even the guy who had been keeping guard on Anna, and who was probably still unconscious. But they had stirred up a hornet's nest.

It wouldn't take the small army of men de Rocheford had employed very long to exhaust their search of the grounds and decide to check on the cliffs. They needed to be off this peninsula ASAP.

He could feel Anna shivering against him, and his jaw tensed at what she'd been through. He didn't know if she'd been hurt yet, but he would find out every last detail. As much as he wanted to make de Rocheford and Seber pay personally for what they'd done, his need for revenge had to be secondary. His objective had been to get Anna back, and he had achieved that. She was now right where he wanted her—in his arms. The police would take control of the situation, and Ray would be more than happy to see to it that justice was done. As of tonight, de Rocheford had officially lost everything, including his freedom. He would never come near Anna again, never intrude on her life or threaten her. It wasn't nearly enough for Blade, but it would have to do.

When his feet touched the pebbled beach below, Blade lifted Anna from the cliff, stripped the harness from them both, and did what he'd wanted to do when he'd first found her. He jerked his lip microphone down, pulled her into his arms and kissed her, giving vent to his savage relief. Her mouth was soft and willing, her arms tight around his neck, but it wasn't enough. He wanted to pull her closer than his damn body armour allowed, grind himself against her and make the kiss last for a long, long time.

When Seber had walked in on them as they were leaving, Blade had been certain he was on his way to execute her, panicking because the police had been camped at the gate, demanding entrance. He had got to her first, but it had been too close, their timing off because they had searched the wrong house. Reluctantly, he lifted his mouth and forced himself to release her.

One by one, the men jumped down onto the beach. Carter began collecting the harnesses. Ben and West dragged the boat to the water and aimed it into the waves.

The sound of rotors beat on the air; light scythed the night, arcing across the edge of the cliffs, then receding, as the police chopper swung closer to the main house. A voice from a loudhailer commanded the men above to put down their weapons and lie on the ground.

Blade pulled Anna with him to the boat, allowing himself a cold smile as the spotlight was kept scrupulously away from the cliffs.

The heavy beat of the helicopter masked the sound of the outboard motor as it coughed to life, then settled into a low buzz as the boat moved into the choppy surf. Seconds later, they were past the mouth of the shallow cove, forging out to sea.

Waves slapped at the sides, sending spray flying, so that they were drenched within moments. The inflatable was fast, but didn't have the seaworthiness of a boat with a deeper hull. It skimmed the surface instead of cutting, and was buffeted by both waves and wind.

Blade pulled Anna between his legs, wrapping his arms around her to give her maximum body contact and cushion her against the bouncing jolt as they hit each swell. Her chilled skin worried him. She had been shut in that cold room for hours, wearing only jeans, sneakers and his shirt, and now she was getting wet. He peeled off his vest, then removed his shirt and put it on Anna, before slipping the vest back on. The extra layer wasn't enough, but it was better than nothing.

She was still too quiet, and he didn't know if it was because of whatever they had drugged her with, or if she was in shock. The unnatural calm worried Blade more than anything else since he had found her alive. Apart from the moments when she had mistaken him for one of her captors and tried to take him out, then escape, she had docilely done everything he had demanded.

It was calmer when they got away from the shore, the choppy waves subsiding into lazy swells. Thirty minutes later, the inflatable nosed into the small bay where their vehicles were parked.

Anna accepted Blade's helping hand out of the boat, her sneakers splashing in the water, because she had to clamber over the side rather than the bow. As soon as they'd surfed in on a wave, the blond guy, Carter, had leaped out and swung the nose of the boat toward the sea. She understood why, as the next wave rolled in and simply lifted the bow. If the stern had been pointing that way, the boat would have been swamped.

They had all pulled their balaclavas off now, to reveal faces savagely striped with camouflage paint and some kind of microphone attachment that curved round from their ears to their mouths. Blade made quick introductions, and she found herself shaking hands and fielding grinning comments with these strange midnight men who had rescued her.

Blade led her to where the Jeep was parked and stripped off the heavy vest he had been wearing, leaving his torso bare. He pulled out a blanket and wrapped it around her shoulders.

Within minutes, the boat had been deflated and loaded onto the back of a black truck, the motor stowed and all the climbing equipment packed away. As they worked, the men traded amiable insults, discussed the possibility that they *could* have done some fishing if only they had thought to pack a trolling line, and voiced disgust over the poor form of a prominent football team, which would likely plunge the whole country into a depression overnight if it didn't win next week's game.

Any sign that the men had been involved in anything other than a little night fishing had been erased. There were even rods sprouting from rod holders on the back of the truck. Anna shook her head in dazed disbelief. Except for the efficient way they had dealt with the boat and their gear, and the lethal-looking black clothing, they could have been any group of men out on a night fishing trip. But, of course, they weren't.

"You're SAS."

The cheerful banter stopped. There was a moment of considered silence, the weight of four gazes falling on her.

The reality of what had just taken place sank in. Blade could have died; they all could have died. She had noticed that nowhere, at any time, had she seen any evidence of guns. The only weapon any of them appeared to have carried was a knife.

A knife. The fishing rods looked deadlier than the knives.

"I brought you some clothes."

Anna looked blankly at Blade as he pushed a towel into her hands. He hadn't answered her question; none of them had. They had simply gone back to their tasks as if she hadn't spoken.

"You need to get changed into some dry clothes."

Or what? she thought acidly. *She would catch her death?*

There was a chorus of goodbyes in guy-shorthand, an invitation for Blade and Anna to drop around at McCabe's place and watch one football team cream another while they knocked back a few cold ones. The blond guy, Carter, clapped Blade on the shoulder, grinned and winked at her; then they all piled into the truck and drove away, red tail-lights winking, fishing rods clattering in their rod-holders.

Blade pulled a small canvas pack from the Jeep and extracted a pile of fresh clothing. Without asking her, he began unbuttoning the two layers of wet shirt she was wearing.

If Anna's hands hadn't felt so clumsy with cold, she would have batted his hands away. "You didn't have a gun," she said tonelessly.

He undid the last button and peeled both shirts off in one go, tossing them aside. "None of us had guns."

Her palms slammed into his chest.

He stumbled back against the Jeep, catching her hands and pulling her with him, so she ended up falling against him. It was a neat trick.

Anna glared into his lazily amused face, incensed beyond any thought of control. "You came after me armed with only a knife!"

His arms went around her, hugging her in close, so that his heat wrapped her far more effectively than the blanket had. "You got a problem with that?" he murmured.

She resisted the urge to wrap her arms around his waist, to bury her face against his shoulder. He knew he could melt her with a touch, knew it and traded on it. She tilted her chin, which brought her eyes level with his mouth. "Yeah. A big problem. *They* had guns."

"They didn't get to use them."

"What if something had gone wrong? What if—"

His mouth dipped, cutting her short with a soft, cajoling pressure. "There was no time for anything else, and no other way."

He briefly explained their reasoning and the involvement of the police, but if he'd thought that was going to calm her down, he was *so* wrong.

"You deliberately walked into a trap."

"No. We used Henry's trap to our advantage. We gathered information, formulated and carried out a strategy. It was a calculated risk, but it worked." His voice hardened. "They got hold of you because *I* slipped up. I wasn't waiting for a more conventional solution. I wanted you out of there."

Anna almost flinched at his abrupt change in tone from soft cajoling to cold command. He had made a mistake and rectified it, at the same time taking down both Seber and de Rocheford. He had done it all in one stroke, when most people would have seen each separate problem as difficult—and all three as definitely in the "too-hard" basket. Blade had taken the problem apart and found a solution, controlled all the components in the game. She knew he was trained for this, that he was obviously very, very good at it, but even so, she was still reeling from the terrible risk he had taken. A risk that he had calculated like an equation.

She had already known about this side of Blade. That streak of ruthlessness, that need for control that bordered on cold calculation, was as much a part of him as the charm and playfulness, the burning sensuality—but the abyss between the two was alarming.

She loved Blade, every exciting, irresistible, complex part of him, but right now she felt like she was walking a shaky bridge that straddled that abyss. The passionate part of him wanted her, but what happened when the cold, logical, in-control part of Blade could no longer stomach her psychic talent? The uncontrollable invasion of privacy she represented?

What happened if she did to Blade what she had unwittingly done to Henry? Would he look at her with that wintry cold in his eyes as he told her it was over?

They had shared a great deal, but they had only spent one night together. She loved him with every particle of her being, but essentially, they were strangers. Intimate strangers.

Then there was that other small detail that kept nagging at her. He didn't need her. The dreams had been all about *her* need, not his. She had called out, and he had answered.

She realised that the inner cold that had crept deeper with the years didn't have anything to do with de Rocheford or the way she had been hunted, it had to do with Blade. He was the only one who could warm her. He was the only one who could banish her loneliness. He was essential to her in some way she didn't quite understand, just as she didn't understand her psychic talent.

The situation reminded her of a delicate orchid she had read about once. The exotic plant required a certain rare nutrient to survive and flourish. If it didn't get that nutrient, it refused to flower, and gradually withered and died. She had reached out for what *she* had needed in her dreams and taken it, regardless of the cost to Blade.

She wondered how she was going to control her need.

She felt like a thief in the night. She felt like some kind of emotional vampire.

Chapter 16

Blade shook her gently. "Anna, what is it?"

His voice was rough with concern. He was still holding her close against him, his arms tight, as if he absolutely did not want to let her go. His body heat warmed her against the night chill, but no amount of winter cold even approached the subzero reality of losing him.

"What will happen to Henry?" she asked, desperate to deflect both his attention and her own fears.

Blade released her, stripped her damp bra off and began shoving her arms into another of his shirts. Automatically, Anna began rolling the dangling sleeves up.

Blade's eyes were slitted and grim as he handled the buttons. "I've had just about enough of Henry. I guess when we're married, I'll be related to the bastard. Brings to mind that saying that you can't pick your relatives."

Anna's chest contracted as if she'd just been kicked. Marriage? She studied his bent head as he went down on his haunches to pull off her sneakers, and a wave of longing swept her, so intense she was dizzy with it. She wanted to reach out and touch his hair, drown in the pure pleasure of simply being able to do so. She had *dreamed* of this, dreamed of Blade…wanted him so much it hurt, but she couldn't just give in and let him sweep her away. She needed to know that he could love her, *all* of her, first. "I haven't said I'll marry you," she said flatly.

Blade went still, then simply started on her jeans, patiently peeling them down and taking her panties with them. He wrapped her in the blanket again, then stripped off his own pants and boots, pulling on fresh jeans and a T-shirt before hustling her into the front seat of the Jeep.

He started the engine and set the heater on full blast, then handed her a thermos of coffee and a huge sandwich consisting of massive slices of bread and equally massive slices of cheese and ham. She drank and chewed, discovering she was ravenous, while he collected all their wet things and stowed them in the back. By the time Blade swung into the driver's seat, her fingers and toes were tingling with warmth, and she was feeling sleepy. Considering that she had spent most of the day asleep, she was disgusted with herself.

She did up her seat belt and folded her arms across her chest, fighting the sudden giddy delight of being alive, of them both being alive. Of finally being free of Henry.

She stared at the bright sweep of headlights picking out the winding road, the fence posts. She was free.

She didn't have to run anymore. Henry and Seber would be in custody by now.

It was hard to take in, especially when she considered that if Blade hadn't found her in Ambrose Park and chosen to involve himself in all this, she would be dead.

"How many times have you saved my life?" she rasped.

"I haven't been counting." Blade flashed her a slow grin, caught her fingers and drew them to his mouth.

Oh, yes, he was arrogant and magnificent, and too damn cocky for his own good, and she knew she was going to have a hard job resisting him, if she could resist him at all. Her instincts as a child had been accurate. Blade was a knight—her knight. She just hadn't realised he was also a ruthless conqueror.

She must have slept. When she awoke, they were bumping along a rutted road, and as they came around a bend, she saw a house that looked like a castle keep, stone-walled and stark against a moonlit expanse of ocean. Mist rose off the surface of the water, long tendrils flowing on the night air, sinking into dips and hollows, condensing on the massive walls so that they gleamed like wet mail in the moonlight.

There was an enormous sweep of barren ground surrounding the building, which she realised wasn't old at all, but starkly modern. The bare dirt would one day be an emerald sweep of lawn. She could almost see the graceful trees and shrubs, the riotous beds of flowers, which would complement the lawn and soften the solid, uncompromising lines of the stonework.

The house stood alone and lonely, incomplete, yet

compelling, a thing of fairy tales and myths, as isolated in this quiet valley as a fierce eagle in its eyrie.

Blade pulled to a stop in front of a massive door that looked like it had been constructed to withstand a siege. He opened the Jeep's glovebox and grabbed a flashlight and a set of keys.

Anna unclipped her seat belt. "Where are we?" The question seemed mundane. She felt she should have been asking, "*When* are we?"

"My house."

It figured, she thought, as she pushed her door open and climbed down to the gravelled drive, still holding the blanket around her shoulders. Blood will out. Blade Lombard was a reaver from way back, with a reaver's instincts. The house shouted out who and what he was loud and clear. He would take, and he would hold.

He unlocked the huge double doors, which swung inward on well-oiled hinges. Then he strode back to the Jeep, extracted his pack from the rear, locked the vehicle, then came around to take her arm.

Anna didn't protest, soaking up even this small touch with a hungry delight. She felt strangely light-headed, filled with a nervous energy. And scared. *His house.* Already she could feel the pull of it somewhere deep inside her. This keep of a house was so achingly like Blade, an extension of his personality. She didn't care what it was like inside; she loved it already.

Oh, yeah, she was scared. She didn't want to find more things about him to love, to weave him any deeper into the very fabric of her being, because she couldn't afford to trust in the fairy tale. She had spent a lifetime dreaming, fantasizing—had even chosen to spend her leisure time creating fantasies on a page—

but reality for her had always been gritty, almost too real. Only with Blade had the fantasy and reality become inextricably entwined.

The hall was massive and high ceilinged, the floor paved with what looked like flagstones and probably were.

He led her into a huge, bare room, the lounge. There was a fireplace big enough to walk into, an easel in one corner and the smell of linseed oil in the air, and a mattress on the floor piled with pillows and a sleeping bag. He showed her where the nearest bathroom was, leaving her with the torch. When she walked back into the lounge, he had a fire blazing, and candlelight flickered from several heavy candelabra.

He rose to his feet, pulling off his T-shirt in one fluid movement, letting it drop to the floor. ''It'll be a little primitive until the power's hooked up. The electricians are still working on the wiring.''

He took the torch from her, switched it off and put it beside the makeshift bed she knew they were going to share—for tonight, anyway. Anna eyed him uncertainly. His declaration that they were going to get married still hung between them, impossible and unresolved.

He checked out the fading bruise on her forehead, the scratch on her arm, undoing the grubby bandage and tossing it in the fire. He was quiet, restrained, and that set Anna even more on edge.

He was staring into her eyes now, his black gaze almost distant. ''Do you know what you were drugged with?''

''Something on a cloth first. Ether, maybe. Then, later, sleeping pills.''

"Do you feel nauseous or dizzy?"

She shook her head. What she felt was nervous and crazy. She was going to be sleeping with Blade in that bed—they were going to make love—and she didn't think she could stand to be pushed any closer to him if she was going to end up losing him.

"Good." He crossed his arms over his chest, his eyes narrowing to glittering slits. "Then now is as good a time as any for you to tell me why you can't marry me when I know damn well that you love me."

"Because I don't think it will work," she said bluntly. "How can it? The whole thing has been a—a fantasy. You can have any woman you want. Why would you want me beyond some kind of novelty value?" There, she'd said part of it, even if she was holding back on the worst bit. "There were the dreams, and then there was all the danger. Nothing about our relationship has been normal."

He gave her a disbelieving look. "And you think that if we have a 'normal' relationship neither of us will be interested?"

"I didn't say that. When I said 'I love you,' I meant it."

"What happens if you're pregnant? When we made love, I didn't wear a condom."

She went weak at the thought. The mere idea of growing Blade's baby inside her filled her with an aching hunger. "Even if there's a baby," she said in a voice so flat and toneless she hardly recognised it as her own, "we don't have to get married. People don't, these days."

He dropped his hands to his sides and stepped toward her, so close that his heat and scent, the hot wash of his vitality, swamped her. "If there's a baby, we'll be married," he stated.

His jaw was set, his eyes hooded and burning like live coals. "And while we're clearing the air," he said silkily, "what took you so long to call me?"

It took a moment for what he meant to sink in. "Call you?"

"Yeah, as in *Starship Enterprise* to Earth, beam me up, Scotty."

Her hands curled into fists at his sarcasm. "I've never beamed anyone up yet."

"Don't sweat it," he muttered. "There's still time."

"I know I'm...different, but I'm not *that* strange."

"Couldn't prove it by me." Blade wheeled away from her and stalked to the centre of the room, as if he needed to work off some of his restless tension. Firelight gleamed on his broad shoulders as he spun to face her. "Most women I know *like* to call me. They appreciate that I'm interested in them, that I care about their safety. They would love to know that I was worried about them. Some of them would even get a thrill out of knowing I'm primed and ready to kill for them." He eyed her broodingly. "Maybe I've been spoiled, but that's the way it's been for me so far."

Anna eyed him warily. He had *wanted* her to make contact with her mind?

Blade's mention of all the women he'd known, and probably made love to, in the past stung. If he'd wanted to hurt her, he couldn't have picked a better way than letting her know she was just one of many.

Her temper stirred. The "many" probably stretched into an army of satisfied women. "Maybe you should go and call one of those women right now, if they're all so hot for you," she snapped. "And I 'called' you just as soon as I could."

He eyed her moodily, his bad temper a tangible presence in the cavernous room. "It wasn't soon enough for me."

"You...didn't mind that I—"

"I was *waiting* for the damn call. It killed me inside when it didn't come."

He prowled toward her. His hands landed on her shoulders, his grip firm. She got the impression he would have liked to shake her and was barely managing to hold himself in check.

"I was drugged," she said dazedly. "When I woke up, I thought about calling you, but I didn't want to put you in danger if there was no need."

No need. Blade listened to her with mounting fury. He had been imagining Anna hurt, bleeding, maybe even dead.

No, not dead, he decided savagely. He would have known if she was dead.

Acknowledging the link between them only fueled his temper, reminding him that for years he had been forced to watch while, time and again, she escaped death by the skin of her teeth. But this time, when he had been ready and able to save her, she had been debating whether or not she needed his help!

"So what made you call?" His voice was little more than a whisper. He was afraid that if he allowed any more volume out, he would end up yelling.

"Henry had organised a trap. They were going to kill you. I couldn't let them do that."

Oh, yeah, he could see her logic now. "So you called me for my own protection."

"Yes."

He surveyed the tilt of her chin, the stubborn set to her mouth, the faintly narrowed gaze that hinted at the redheaded temper he knew lived under all that frosty control. Satisfaction curled inside him. He was finally getting under her skin. "Did it ever occur to you that I might not want to be protected from Henry?"

Her eyes widened fractionally.

"I know this is probably an old-fashioned notion," he continued softly, "but then, despite the way the tabloids paint me, I'm an old-fashioned kind of guy. In my version of a perfect world, *I* get to slay the dragon, and *I* get to protect the woman I love. That kind of thing is important to me."

She didn't nod, didn't move, just stared at him as if he'd sprouted horns.

Blade's jaw clenched even tighter. He was dying inside by inches, but he couldn't stop now. "One of my fields of expertise is hostage recovery. I've snatched a British diplomat from a South American compound crawling with trigger-happy militia. I've crawled through an underground sewer and penetrated a city building in an Arab state to rescue some of our own men who had been taken prisoner and tortured. I have done a lot of things that could be construed as hazardous to my health. On that scale, de Rocheford and his sidekick, Seber, qualify as little more than a pain in the ass. For years you've called out to me," he said grimly, "and I haven't been able to answer. *This time* I was able to do something. *This time* I could save you. Now do you understand what it did to me to wait?"

"The other reason I didn't want to call you," she

said woodenly, "was because I was afraid you wouldn't...like it."

"Not like it?" He swore beneath his breath. So that was what was wrong! Relief flooded him. "I don't understand how you do it. Hell, I don't understand how *I* pick up whatever it is you do, but I don't care. Baby, in future, if you need to, you will call me at any time of the night or day, is that clear?"

"Yes."

She didn't believe him. She was still shutting him out, pulling that damn self-sufficiency she'd got so comfortable with around her like a cloak.

Well, he'd had enough. He had held back, played the gentleman as much as he was able, intent on giving her time to get over the shock of being kidnapped and incarcerated, but the consideration and coddling hadn't helped; they had made things worse. Then he had muddied the waters further by losing his temper.

For a man who prided himself on knowing how to deal with women, he was making a mess of this. He should have followed his damn instincts all along.

In the dreams they'd shared, Anna had demanded his attention in a sensual, completely feminine way, enticing him to the point of madness, until his control had disintegrated and he had given her what she needed: his utter, focused attention. When he was buried inside her, he had known exactly where he stood with her; he had known she was his. The act had been raw and primitive, stripped to its most basic components. There had been no foreplay, precious little afterplay, just a burning need for each other. Existence had narrowed to what they shared together—and he knew now that what they had shared had gone far deeper than any physical joining.

He began unbuttoning her shirt.

"What are you doing?"

"I'm stripping you naked. Then I'm going to make love to you."

His fingers halted, he met her gaze. He'd thought once that her eyes were shrouded in mist and shadows, but he knew her better now. The mist and shadows hid uncertainty and the same terrible need that burned through him. He was staking his whole future that he wasn't wrong. "That is," he said quietly, "if you're still interested."

"I've always been interested. I was afraid you might not stay interested."

His breath caught on a surge of elation. He'd never been vulnerable emotionally, never been unsure with a woman. Sometimes it seemed that he'd led a charmed existence; everything that he had wanted, he had generally got. Anna was the exception to the rule, and he wanted her more than he had ever wanted anyone or anything. He knew in that moment that if he didn't have her, his life would be flat, empty.

She knew him. Knew the needs that seethed at his core and that he had never unleashed with anyone but her. She had seen who he was, known who he was for years, and reveled in it, demanded more. The dilemma of control versus passion dissolved in that instant, canceled out by the simple fact that Anna was *his,* his mate, the woman who matched him and complemented him in every way. He didn't have to control or hide what he was from her; all he had to do was love her.

He tossed her shirt aside, picked her up and carried

her across to the mattress, laying her down on top of his sleeping bag. It was crude, as far as beds went, but he would make it up to her later. He had plans for a massive four-poster, the kind of bed whole dynasties were founded in. He looked forward to the founding process.

With satisfaction, he saw that her shield of remoteness had been replaced by wary surprise and the same bone-deep longing that was burning him from the inside out. He eyed the splay of her limbs with satisfaction, the silky tumble of her hair and the solemn mystery of her eyes. For the first time since he'd met her, he knew he had her full attention. He meant to hold her attention for a very long time.

There would be no more evasions, no more hiding. No more tiptoeing around her. He understood why she was so skittish. She was worried about his reaction to her psychic talent, and she needed to be sure of him— but he was every bit as hungry for that certainty. She had haunted him, shared his dreams, called out to him when she needed him. Now he needed the certainty of knowing that she would stay with him, be with him.

His hands shook as he tore off his jeans.

With the candlelight and shadows it was like plunging into one of the dreams, only this time it was more urgent, more intense. He had a frightening thought that if he didn't win her now, he never really would, and he couldn't bear to lose her. She had brought a flood of richness to his life. He was like a blind man who had just discovered colours, their special link, strange as it was, just another layer in the richness.

If he wanted to pull the response he wanted from her, he would have to use what he had learned in the dreams—that he wasn't nearly as civilised as he had thought, that somewhere buried deep in his psyche were the same primitive needs that had driven his reaving ancestor to take hold of what he wanted. The dreams must have been prophetic, he thought, as he lowered himself to the bed, control spiraling away even before he touched her. This was much more his style.

Anna gasped at the first touch. In the candlelight, with his hair a tangled mane clinging to his damp shoulders, dark eyes slitted with intent, Blade looked as sensual and untamed as he had in her dreams.

His mouth brushed hers, startlingly soft, warm, his breath washing her cheek. He moved lower, his hair trailed like warm satin over her skin and the musky, hot scent of him filled her nostrils.

He reared up, looming over her, reminding her of the moment, several nights ago, when she had opened her eyes in the ditch and seen him for the first time. Firelight limned his shoulders now, the fluid shift of sleek muscles turning his skin to molten gold.

He picked up her hand and placed it over his heart. "I need you...here."

For an odd, suspended moment, Anna couldn't move, couldn't think, as if his simple action and words had paralysed her inside. His hand tightened on hers as if he would press her hand deep into his flesh, and all the pent-up emotion she'd stamped on and suppressed burst free, and with the release, something else happened...like the ripping away of a veil. Suddenly she could feel the extremity of his need, the fierce inner hope, that matched her own. He loved her. More...he needed her. The moment was as pure and golden as the glow of the firelight that spread through the room.

He wasn't an angel, she thought—he had never been an angel. He was, quite simply, *hers*.

"And here," he said with a wry groan, guiding her hand lower.

Anna's fingers closed around him, and he came to her in a lithe flow, as bonelessly graceful as a big cat.

He let her guide him, then began entering her, the penetration a slow hot burn of pleasure as her body stretched to accommodate him. Anna shivered in delight, wrapping herself around him as his heat poured through her and the firelight flickered around them in a mellow nimbus of soft light.

He caught her face between his hands, and his hair fell in a curtain around them, enclosing them in heat and darkness. "I need you," he stated bluntly. "I love you. If I have to shackle you to my bed, I'll do it. There'll be no more running away. I want you here beside me, so that if anything happens, I can deal with it. It's driven me crazy for years that I couldn't reach out and touch you. I *want* to reach out and touch you any time I feel like it. That means we get married. ASAP. If you want a big church wedding, we can do that later, but I want the paperwork done and that ring on your finger this week. Have you got that?"

Anna shimmied beneath his hold, and he groaned hoarsely. He was supporting most of his weight on his arms, but she was pinned beneath him, and he was buried deep inside her as if he felt the need to anchor her to his bed. Wonder pulsed through her—she wasn't going anywhere unless he threw her out.

A long time later, Anna moved restlessly in sleep, caught in the dark current of a dream that swept her

along and threatened to pull her beneath the surface
where there was no air and no light penetrating, where
it was dark and cold and terribly still. She fought the
current, fought the cold, crying out in protest.

The answer when it came was a low, crooning rumble she turned toward instinctively. The man, for it was
a man, was like fire. The warmth from his body poured
over her, beating back the cold, and that low, hypnotic
voice continued to cajole, pulling her from the dream.

Her eyes flickered open. Blade was cradling her, his
shoulders outlined by the dying glow of the fire. Her
arms wound around his neck, and she clung to him,
taking the comfort he offered.

"I love you," she whispered into his neck, a rush
of love squeezing her heart so tight she felt like it was
being crushed in her chest.

He continued to croon, telling her how much he
loved her, how much he needed her, how long he'd
waited for her, how lonely he'd been. His voice was
low and rough, almost unbearably tender, and all the
while, he stroked her back, her hair, giving her the
magic of his heat, his touch.

He kissed her, his lips soft and lingeringly sweet,
then he settled her on top of him so she was sprawled
on his chest, and slowly entered her.

Instead of making love, he just held her, the hot
throb of his flesh warming her from the inside out.

"Go back to sleep," he whispered.

He draped the sleeping bag over them both, and
Anna let her eyelids drift closed and her breathing even
out, soothed by the steady beat of his heart, the physical link of penetration. Her last coherent thought was
that somehow Blade had understood that her coldness

had been internal—a deep-seated fear that she would lose him—and he had responded by banishing that fear with the only thing that could, the overwhelming certainty of his presence.

She awoke to feel him still lodged inside her and fully aroused.

She lay in the dark, enjoying the slow building pleasure of just having him there, aware that Blade, too, was awake and enjoying the same sweet torment. After a period of time his hands closed on her hips, his thighs pushing up and out, parting her legs until she straddled him. Anna gasped at the abrupt depth of his penetration.

"Better?" he murmured.

Anna levered herself up fully, the puffy softness of the sleeping bag falling away. She rose up, then slid back down in slow increments. She couldn't speak, could barely think; the sensation was almost too intense to bear.

Blade's hands tightened; a low satisfied groan rumbled from deep in his belly. "Oh, yeah, that's it. Just *there*."

The dying glow from the fire illuminated the room, dim light catching the muscular beauty of the torso beneath her hands, the wild mane of black hair spread across the pillow, the darkness of Blade's eyes fixed on her as if, even now, he was afraid she would shimmer into mist and disappear. She rode him slowly and for a long time, utterly absorbed by the heavy fullness of him inside her, the novelty of having his big body sprawled beneath her—hers to play with, hers to love— the flex of sweaty muscle beneath her hands, the shudders that shook through him every time she took him deep.

His hands came up to cup her breasts, and she lost her train of thought as the rough pads of his fingers caressed nipples that were already tightly beaded. She was sensitive to his lightest touch, her flesh tender and aching with a sweet heat, as if she would burst at the next light brush.

His fingers tightened, and hot pleasure burst through her, taking her by storm, so that her whole body tensed, her heart pounded, and her head swam. Her vision receded, as if she were caught in the whirling centre of a storm, blind to everything but Blade. She felt the moment he lost the battle for control. He arched, his hands clasping her firmly against him as he drove deep. He went rigid, trembling against her, his head flung back with a hoarse groan, and she felt the hot, pulsing flood of his release.

No condom again, she thought hazily, as she collapsed on his chest and he gathered her in close.

It was dawn when Anna next awoke to find herself pinned to the mattress by an arm slung possessively over her middle. The fire was no more than a smouldering pile of embers. At some point in the night, Blade had opened up the sleeping bag, turning it into a quilt, but he was so hot to sleep with that, in the end, they'd pushed it down until it was bunched around their hips.

She turned her head on the pillow and looked directly into Blade's warm, intent gaze. Anna remembered something he'd said last night. She touched his stubbled jaw. He looked wild and uncivilised, a dissolute barbarian prince, with his jaw so dark and the earring glinting in the tangled mane of his hair, and she trembled on the edge of an incredulous smile. "You've *never* taken a girlfriend home to meet your family?"

"Never." For the first time Blade allowed himself to put into words the stark truth that had confused, irked and tormented him for years. "I was looking for you. If I couldn't find you, I wasn't going to have anyone."

Chapter 17

"So this is Anna Tarrant."

Ray shook the hand of the woman who had been the cause of all the ruckus. She was small and very attractive, with a mouth to go to war over, and the kind of mesmerising eyes that made him want to keep on looking.

He caught the hard edge of Lombard's gaze and backed off fast. No sense in buying into any more trouble; he'd already seen enough this week to last him. The past few days he'd been hip deep in politicians and slick lawyers, all trying to save de Rocheford's ass. It was a lost cause, but that didn't stop the legal vultures from feeding off the carcass for as long as they could, although he didn't know where de Rocheford stood with the money any longer. Technically he now owned very little.

Anna placed her briefcase on the interview desk and

began removing the small items of her past. An officer catalogued each item and bagged it. Blade hovered protectively as the interview proceeded and she told her story in simple chronological order, ending with de Rocheford's last attempt to kill her.

"I escaped," she finished baldly.

Ray sat back in his chair and folded his arms across his chest. This was the part he knew he wasn't going to like. "How?"

"Seber came into the room they'd locked me in. I got away, then climbed down the cliff to the beach. There was a boat with a motor. I came ashore at a beach with a boat ramp, a little further up the coast. I called Blade. He came and got me."

Ray sighed at Anna's simplistic series of statements. He had no doubt that each one contained its own version of the truth. "Have you got anything you want to add to that explanation?"

"No."

Blade's arm settled about her shoulders. "My fiancée's safe," he said softly. "Surely that's the most important thing."

Ray met Blade's bland gaze and didn't push any further. He knew what Blade had done; knew and respected his reasons, even if he couldn't condone any of it. He decided that Anna's simple series of statements was all he ever wanted to know about what had happened at the de Rocheford estate—on the record or off.

He ended the official interview and began outlining the prosecution proceedings. "Seber's a practical man: he talked. And once he started talking, he didn't stop. The man is certifiably weird. Not only did he imper-

sonate a police officer, he kept police-style records on
all his clients and anyone else who attracted his attention in the course of his 'duties.' We've got Seber and
de Rocheford on one count of murder—the lawyer,
Emerson Stevens. Seber also implicated de Rocheford
in the kidnapping and attempted murder of Miss Tarrant.''

Ray shook his head in incredulity at Seber's cold-
blooded efficiency. ''He taped all his conversations
with his clients, just in case something went wrong.''

''Henry killed my mother, too,'' Anna said flatly.

Ray was caught in the net of her gaze again. He
frowned. There was something about her eyes, aside
from that luminous grey colour. For a moment there
he'd got the distinct impression she had looked...not
through him, but *into* him.

She lifted her brows, and he realised he'd been staring.

Incredibly, he felt his cheeks heat. ''Have you, uh,
got any evidence to support that statement?''

''Henry told me he gave her sleeping pills when she
was already on some other medication,'' she said in a
low voice. ''She simply never woke up. Seber may be
able to confirm the allegation. I think he was listening
at the door when Henry told me about giving her the
pills.''

Ray was hardly surprised. ''We're already investi-
gating that angle,'' he admitted, and suppressed a grin.
He would go talk to Seber again; he could hardly wait.
The man was like Father Christmas; his goody sack
was solving half the crimes in the city.

He rose from his chair and shook hands with both
Anna and Blade. ''With what we've got from Seber,

we shouldn't have any problems getting convictions. He collected evidence by the book.''

Ray strolled to the door, grasped the handle, but didn't open it immediately. He stared at the wood grain as if it were utterly fascinating. ''Seber also nailed a number of petty criminals. One of them was the manager of Joe's Bar and Grill. Apparently he was running a brothel out of the restaurant. A couple of the girls confirmed everything.''

His ears went pink at exactly how much they'd confirmed. The one with the husky voice…what was her name? Nita. She had sunk Rafferty's boat with detailed accounts of every transaction, practically since the dawn of time. The woman should have been an accountant. ''We went to pick Rafferty up, but unfortunately, we haven't been able to book him yet. Apparently he's been falsifying employment records and evading taxes. The tax investigators got there first and gave him a heart attack. He's in hospital and probably wishes he were dead, but the poor bastard's not critical.''

Epilogue

Anna Lombard strode through the crowd thronging the newly opened casino in a grey, glittering sheath that looked more like moonlight and mist than the delicately beaded moire silk that it was.

Addie Carson paused to admire the sleek young woman with the swath of silky, coppery hair tumbling past her waist. She nudged her sister in the ribs. "Sadie, get a load of that dress. Don't you think she looks like something out of a fairy tale?"

Sadie turned, wondering what Addie had seen that was so fascinating it had drawn her away from a sure streak on her favourite slot machine. "Yep." She squinted. "Filled out some. Not surprising, with that big stud hovering over her, watching her every move. I've seen him feed her himself if he doesn't think she's eaten enough."

Just then Blade Lombard glided through the crowd

and laid a possessive hand on the small of his wife's back. He looked big and handsome and wild, his black stallion's mane of hair as glossy as midnight satin under the lights. He turned his head, and the barbaric gleam of the jewel at his ear caught the lights, making him look even more untamed. Against him, his wife looked willowy, and utterly feminine.

The contrast, the way they looked together, made something catch in the sisters' throats. The glance the couple shared was so private, as if there were no one else in the room but the two of them. Both sisters were transfixed by the odd notion that, for a brief moment, they had been allowed a glimpse into something beyond the norm, a moment that was intensely personal—and more spellbinding.

"Oh my," Addie said wistfully.

"Quiet," Sadie muttered, her mind focusing on another subject entirely: Blade Lombard's tight rear end. "I'm concentratin'."

Addie's breath hitched in her throat. "Did you see that?" she muttered. "She squeezed his…"

"Butt."

"Sadie!"

"I'm a modern woman," Sadie grumped. "I know what I saw, and I know what it's called. Just wish I'd had access to one like that."

Addie sighed. "Makes you feel like you missed something on the way, doesn't it?" An image of her beloved but long ago deceased husband lying at home on the couch, television remote practically sutured to one hand, passed very briefly through her mind. Her Harvey had had his moments, enough of them that she could still blush remembering, but still...

Sadie began fussing with the fit of her dress. "Reckon I'll go check on those Fa'alau boys, see how they're going with the security. Tony's been asking my advice on account of this is a lot different from working at a video parlour."

Addie snorted. "If Blade thinks they can handle the job, then they probably don't need your help."

Sadie adjusted her pearls and made a beeline for the entrance to the main gaming floor and the two burly men with the remote, watchful eyes. She eyed the fit of Tony's tux approvingly, completely ignoring his son, Mike. Yessir, he looked dangerous, like a hit man from a movie she'd seen once.

His gaze connected with hers, and he smiled, the special, soft smile that made her heart thump in her chest. Sadie smiled back at him, almost tripping on the hem of her long gown. It had cost her a small fortune, and the result had been worth it, but she would still kill to be back in her jeans.

She had been going to talk about security. Not that Tony was likely to be taken in by any of the smooth characters cruising the tables. Just one look at his dark eyes was enough to give her little shivers up and down her spine. He might have grey in his hair and a limp, but he was one fine figure of a man.

The hell with security. They'd been smiling at each other long enough. She was going to ask him for a date.

Blade tucked his wife in close against his side. "How do you feel?" he murmured, bending to nuzzle her hair. The light, flowery scent of her made his pulse jump. With a sense of amused inevitability, he felt his sex stir.

Anna smiled, her grey eyes losing their mystery and gaining a teasing sparkle that made him even hungrier to have her alone.

"You keep asking me that. I'm fine."

"I have a vested interest in my wife," he murmured as he guided her toward a small club that adjoined the main casino floor. There was a band playing slow dance music, and he wanted to hold his wife in his arms. "And my new business partner."

With de Rocheford and Seber both serving substantial prison terms, and Anna's identity and inheritance restored, her life had changed dramatically. She was now a businesswoman, and she'd taken to it like the proverbial duck to water—her talent for reading people giving her a definite edge. Anna was also a partner in the horse stud, and had a family share in Lombards. Blade hadn't needed to do either of the last two things, because Anna's income was already substantial, but he had wanted to give her the security of being closely bound to both him and his family.

She still had the occasional bad dream, but they just about had those beaten. Blade's remedy was simple and basic; he warmed her up inside and out. The strategy had worked so well, he'd wondered about the last couple of wake up calls; Anna hadn't felt the least bit cold.

Her hand slid across his belly as they strolled onto the dance floor, fingers lightly massaging. Blade's chest expanded on a sharp intake of air as he pulled her into his arms, but he let her play, because she damn well needed to play. When he'd found out why she'd run so hard and for so long from Henry, he'd nearly gone crazy. The bastard was lucky he'd been locked up. Anna had gradually emerged from the shell she'd used to protect herself. Like a butterfly emerging from its chrysalis, she'd expanded on that serious, haunted personality that had grabbed him so deep and hard, and spread wings that glittered and scintillated and grabbed him even tighter.

He'd done some research into the Montague family and their women. They were avowed to have powers. Dangerous powers.

Didn't he know it. His ghost lady was a damn tease.

Jack danced past, with Milly held as closely as they could manage with her pregnancy. Milly was wearing a glowing smile and a fire-engine-red dress that cheerfully flaunted the curve of her belly. The entire Lombard family was here tonight, and most of them were dancing. Gray and Sam had a corner to themselves, and Cullen and Rachel had staked out their own piece of territory. Blade's parents were doing a stately turn on the floor, and his sister, Roma, had an amiable Carter in tow, his expression long-suffering as she drove him crazy with questions about exactly what it was he did on his undercover missions.

Anna lifted both arms around Blade's neck, snuggling against his chest so they didn't so much dance as sway together. Idly, she began to stroke his nape with a rhythmic, flexing motion.

"Keep doing that," he muttered, "and you're likely to get tossed over my shoulder."

"Finally." She slipped one hand down his chest,

found the hard, sensitive point of his nipple beneath his dress shirt and rubbed.

Blade's heart almost stopped, then pounded hard and fast. He broke out in a sweat, his arousal instant and cataclysmic. He had to have her, and he didn't have much time.

"That's it," he growled, soft and desperate. "There were no witches in the Montague family. They were all torturers."

He caught Anna's unrepentant face with his hands and kissed her deep and long—just as he knew she wanted him to.

A camera flashed, capturing the unruly flare of passion. It would be all over the papers tomorrow, he thought hazily, not caring, as he picked Anna up and strode to the private lift that went directly to their penthouse suite, ignoring the interested spectators scurrying aside to allow him passage.

"Hit the combination," he commanded. "My hands are busy."

The lift swished open. He stepped inside. Another camera flashed as the doors closed. Blade lowered Anna to her feet, pinned her against the wall of the lift and kissed her again.

He felt her searching for the key card in his pants pocket, an action that took an inordinately long time and necessitated movements above and beyond the call of duty.

Eventually, the lift began its smooth ascent. Seconds later, it came to an abrupt halt in mid-climb. Anna had hit the stop button. Blade knew in that moment that they weren't going to make it out of the lift any time soon.

Anna had no intention of letting Blade out of the lift for at least an hour. The Lombard family suite was full, presently hosting a clutch of Blade's nieces and nephews, and a couple of demonic young cousins, all overseen by his Aunt Sophie. The children and babies were adorable, and Sophie was charming, but there was no privacy. Anna had had enough of sharing her husband; she wanted him to herself.

"This dress is tight," he muttered, a desperate edge to his voice. "You've put on weight."

"The last of the smooth talkers," she murmured. "You really know how to make a lady feel gorgeous."

She nipped at his lobe in delicate reprisal, then grinned when he shuddered with delight.

He grasped her skirt and worked it up over her hips, then stiffened and went still. "You're wearing a suspender belt," he accused.

"I sneaked it on when you weren't looking," she murmured, rubbing her palms over his shirtfront. His chest expanded; heavy muscles tightened.

"Witch." His gaze was possessive and burning with need, but soft, so soft.

"Flatterer," she retorted, no longer worried about her wild Montague genes. Her psychic talents had been catalogued, listed, analysed and measured, as much as anyone was able to measure anything so intangible. She had decided not to share any of her dreams, though; they belonged to her and Blade, and were far too personal for a research paper.

Anna had found out she was special, but not alone. She was, in the latest jargon, an empath—meaning that she could pick up on feelings, emotions. She also had a capacity for mental telepathy, but it appeared to be at its strongest with Blade.

Her link with Blade had the experts baffled, and they had wanted to test him, too, certain that he must have a degree of the same talent, even if it was only minor. Blade had refused point blank, just as he had put his foot down about her participating in an ongoing programme of testing. In his words, Anna was his wife, not some guinea pig. If she wanted to use her powers on anyone, it was going to be on him.

The one thing that had really bothered Anna was what she'd done to Henry when she'd hit out with her mind. They had conducted tests and tried to get her to replicate the effect, but she hadn't been able to do it. She had come to the conclusion that what had happened with Henry had been an aberration, fueled by the years of fear and grief and anguish. During the test, she simply hadn't been able to build up any fury at all; she had been too happy.

She wound her arms around Blade's neck and obligingly wriggled her hips as he peeled her dress up until it bunched at her waist. He leaned down and whispered something bluntly explicit in her ear.

A shiver swept her as she felt the edge of his teeth on the tender join of neck and shoulder. He had called her fat, a witch, and now he had told her what he was about to do to her in a string of very short words.

He lifted her and set her back against the wall of the elevator. Anna heard the rasp of his zipper, shivered as she felt the hot, beguiling stroke of his fingers, then without further preliminaries, he began pushing inside her.

His eyes were hooded, intent, his dark golden skin stretched taut against the strong bones and exotic hollows of his face. And then there was no more time for talking. At least, nothing that could be described as a coherent word.

Hours later, Blade left their bed, pulled from sleep by a dream that had shaken him.

He pushed the doors to the balcony wide and stepped out. The weather was hot, balmy, a soft breeze deliciously cool against his naked skin. He stared at the narrow curve of the moon, riding low against the cityscape, the nascent glimmer of impending dawn in the east.

The power of the dream washed over him again, sending an odd, weakening tremor through him.

"Bad dream?" Anna murmured, coming up behind him, slipping her arms around his waist and hugging in against his back.

Blade turned in her grasp, pulling her close. Fierce elation thrummed through him. He wished he had her to himself closeted at home, closeted to himself; he wouldn't let her out of bed for a week. Sometimes the extent and depth of his love for Anna shook him, but never more so than now. "Uh-uh. Great dream."

Contentment filled Blade as he held his wife—and his future—close, safe, against him.

He didn't know if Anna knew it yet, but she was pregnant.

Maybe he should do some research into his own an-

cestors, he mused. Amongst the brigands and merce-
naries, buccaneers and pirates, he wouldn't be surprised
if he discovered a warlock or two.

* * * * *

INTIMATE MOMENTS®
Silhouette®

presents a riveting 12-book continuity series:

a Year of loving dangerously

Where passion rules and nothing is what it seems...

When dishonor threatens a top-secret agency,
the brave men and women of SPEAR are prepared to
risk it all as they put their lives—and their hearts—
on the line.

Available September 2000:

NIGHT OF NO RETURN
by Eileen Wilks

Hard-edged Alex Bok fought valiantly to keep his emotions
in check when a dangerous undercover assignment reunited
him with the virginal beauty he found irresistible. Could he
accomplish his mission...*and* surrender his heart to love?

*Available only from Silhouette Intimate Moments
at your favorite retail outlet.*

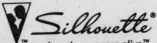

Silhouette®

Where love comes alive™

The hours between dusk and dawn are filled with mystery, danger...and romance.

On sale September...

#1 *New York Times* bestselling author

NORA ROBERTS

brings you four dark and dazzling tales
of passion and peril in

NIGHT TALES

a special 4-in-1 collector's edition containing 4 stories
from her Night series from Silhouette Books.

And also in September

NIGHT SHIELD

a brand-new book in the exciting Night Tales series,
from Silhouette Intimate Moments.

Silhouette®
Where love comes alive™

Celebrate
Silhouette's 20th Anniversary
with *New York Times* bestselling author

LINDA HOWARD

and the long-awaited story of
CHANCE MACKENZIE
in

A GAME OF CHANCE

IM #1021
On sale in August 2000

Hot on the trail of a suspected terrorist, covert intelligence officer Chance Mackenzie found, seduced and subtly convinced the man's daughter, Sunny Miller, to lead her father out of hiding. The plan worked, but then Sunny discovered the truth behind Chance's so-called affections. Now the agent who *always* got his man had to figure out a way to get his woman!

Available at your favorite retail outlet.

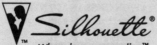

Where love comes alive™

∇INTIMATE MOMENTS®

™ *Silhouette*®

COMING NEXT MONTH

CMN0800